Foreword

It is before the advent of man, and animals are the dominant species. Jethro is a special mouse: a 'Ticklemouse', but he doesn't know it yet.

What starts off as a relatively simple journey to fetch Nana, his wife Hanna's grandmother, and bring her to their home for the winter, takes many unexpected turns.

The adventure really starts when Jethro meets up with Timmo, an ex marine militia sea otter. Timmo is on the trail of the mysterious Raiders who - led by the merciless and sinister General Legin - have abducted his family.

Together the two must face the perils of the predatory Cats, as well as the Raiders and their Weasel helpers, before Jethro discovers his unexpected heritage and aids the redoubtable Timmo in his attempts to rescue his family and stop the Raiders from succeeding in their evil plans.

A catalogue record for this book is available from the
British Library on request.

ISBN: 0-9554288-0-7
ISBN 13:   978 0-9554288-0-7

Published by
Ticklemice Enterprises Ltd www.ticklemice.co.uk
in conjunction with:
Writersworld Limited   www.writersworld.co.uk
9 Manor Close, Enstone, Oxfordshire OX7 4LU

Printed and bound in Great Britain by CPI Antony
Rowe, Eastbourne, East Sussex BN23 6PE

Ticklemice

A story for children to read to
their parents or vice versa.

By

G S Powell

This book is dedicated to:

My wife and children, who put up with and inspire me.

Also to my parents, long since passed on, who always believed in me, and who will stay in my memories.

And finally to my closest friends, who, by definition, may be few in number, but make up for it with the strength of their friendship.

Acknowledgements

Over the last few months I have come to realise that the process of producing a book has at least two parts. Firstly there is the writing, which I take the blame or the credit for; secondly there is turning the manuscript into a finished article available for purchase by the public. With regard to the second part I would like to acknowledge my thanks to the various people, most of whom I have only communicated with by email between August and October of this year, who have been involved in the second part. In chronological order of my 'meeting' them, many many thanks to:

- Graham Cook of Writersworld Ltd., who was the starting point and hub of the whole self-publish process.

- Laurie McAdams of Keygraphic in the USA, who has been incredibly helpful, an absolute pleasure to work with and who produced and designed the cover jacket layout

- Laura Booth who has had the difficult task of trying to edit my version of punctuation

- Jackie Valerio who has produced some sensational illustrations for me, which I feel help to bring the characters to life, and who also contributed to the cover jacket.

G S Powell   October 2006

Chapter 1

'The Beginning'

It all began a long time ago. Not as long ago as when the first stars had hung lantern-like in the deep night sky, but long enough for people to wonder whether it had all really happened or was just a tall tale.

In those days the world looked very different from today's, and the continents were completely unlike ours. Life had begun in the sea and evolved onto the land. The dinosaurs - terrible lizards - had long since disappeared, and animals ruled the Earth, for man had yet to appear on the planet.

The animals were intelligent then and many could speak much as we do today. Such an animal is one of the heroes of our story, which now begins...

Father Ticklemouse, not that he knew he was a Ticklemouse then, was busy making preparations for a long hazardous journey north.

1

Word had come, late in the summer that Nana, Mother Ticklemouse's grandmother was poorly.

With winter coming, a family gathering had been convened, at which Grammy and Grampa, and Father and Mother had decided that the best place for Nana would be with them in their cosy home in the south.

Gem and Ash, the Ticklemice's two mischievous children, were getting ready for bed. At least their parents thought they were. In reality, as usual, they were larking about.

'Come along you two,' hollered Father Ticklemouse up the stairs. 'Get your night clothes on, and into bed. Schooling starts tomorrow, and you won't be at your best if you don't get enough sleep.'

'We are getting ready Dadda,' replied Gem, 'but Ash seems to have disappeared.' she went on, trying to suppress a giggle.

Downstairs Mother Ticklemouse was making up packages of food and supplies, for the first part of Father's journey. These would last him until he reached the City, where he would be able to barter for further provisions, sufficient for the rest of the journey to Nana's little house in the hamlet of Vale.

Mother Ticklemouse was well organised and hardworking, like most mothers, and could not sleep easily unless all her chores were done. She was also worried about Father going away on this journey. He was older than she was, and although reasonably fit for his age, was beginning to be troubled by the odd ache and pain. And then there were the perils of the trek itself; not the least of which were the Cats.

Everyone knows that cats nowadays prey on mice as well as birds and other animals, but long ago the cats were even more cunning and ferocious than they are now, and many was the head of a household who left his home one morning never to be seen again.

Indeed, although he rarely discussed it much with the children, it was because it would have been too dangerous to travel through Cat territory that Father Ticklemouse was unable to visit his three grown up children: Roliver, Anso and Nathan, all of whom lived a long way away, across the sea on the far side of the lands inhabited by the Cats.

The clamour from the rooms above them, together with the thumping sounds of the floor being jumped on and furniture being moved around, became even more irritating.

'Can you go up and deal with them, love?' Mother asked in exasperation. 'You can see how busy I am, and there are still hours to go before bed, with all this and their schooling clothes to get ready for first thing.'

'Alright Mother, I'm on my way,' he replied a little grumpily, as he started up the stairs, going on to exclaim, 'I'm coming to sort you two out!'

By the time he had rounded the top of the stairs all had become silent. Not even a murmur was evident. Father Ticklemouse opened Ash's bedroom door and saw what appeared to be Ash snuggled up in bed. Bending down to give his son a goodnight kiss he heard a rustling behind the curtains and began to look up.

'Gotcha!' .

Two howls of delight burst from his children as they launched themselves like demented birds of prey from either side of the window onto his back.

Father Ticklemouse went down in a heap under their combined momentum, twisting as he fell, so that he ended up on his back with the two young mice on top of him. He could barely move except for his paws, which were trapped slightly under his children's sides. He began to move them in a fluttering random motion, and soon found the youngsters were transformed into helpless laughter as a result, so much so that they were forced to roll off him and beg for him to stop. By this time he was laughing himself and all three lay gasping for breath upon the floor.

'Calm down now you two!' said Father Ticklemouse, stroking their furry foreheads in a soothing gentle motion, 'It won't do to get all excited. You'll never get to sleep!'

Gradually, the young mice quietened and relaxed, as Father Ticklemouse gently cooed:

'Go to sleep my ducks, go to sleep'

'Yes Dadda,' they whispered back drowsily, 'whatever you say Dad.'

Soon they were snoring softly, so Father Ticklemouse decided it would be safe to put them to bed.

As he would need to leave before they awoke the next day, he felt a little sad, so he gave each one a gentle hug and a kiss on the cheek, before making his way back downstairs.

Late into the night he worked with Mother Ticklemouse checking maps and his weather almanac, and stowing various supplies and kit into different sections of his old canvas haversack, for safekeeping and ease of access.

Amongst other things, this included his poacher's travelling fly rod, reel and line, along with some artificial flies, which he knew were deadly. Being able to catch the odd fish or two might be crucial to his survival if his supplies ran low.

The next things to be attached were a small metal stove, a pan, a kettle and two tin cups in case he lost one of the others. These were all secured to the outside of the haversack, by various leather straps.

Father and Mother Ticklemouse finished by cleaning and sharpening an ancient sword and its scabbard, which were said to have belonged to a seafaring ancestor of Father Ticklemouse's and handed down to him by his long dead father.

At last the two adults retired to bed, arms encircled round each other in a tired but loving embrace.

'You will take care won't you, darling?' sighed Mother sleepily.

'Yes, love I'll ...' but he was asleep before he could finish.

Outside, the wind began to stir up, rising to a low howl, and rustling the leaves in the trees. The moon was full, and many many miles away, deep in the dark woods, malevolent creatures began to stir.

Wicked eyes glowed like coals and flared nostrils sought to sniff out the scent of the weak and the vulnerable.

The Cats were abroad as well, hungry and spiteful. Before the night was out they would quench their hunger and their wicked instincts, but only for a day. When the next evening came they would resume their search, covering the land more extensively than usual and straying beyond their normal territory. Swiftly and stealthily, they would proceed in their pursuit for more helpless victims and further sustenance.

Inevitably their path would cross that of Father Ticklemouse, who at this moment slumbered innocently in his comfortable bed. Peacefully, unaware of what the days following had in store for him. Oh dear...!

Chapter 2

'Timmo'

As dawn broke above the hills and woods overlooking the Ticklemouse dwelling, Father Ticklemouse was quietly closing the entrance gate in the palisade fence which surrounded his home. Mother Ticklemouse stood silently waiting for the click of the latch, as she prepared to secure the gate from her side.

They had said their goodbyes after breakfast, amidst hugs and misty eyes, and now Father Ticklemouse strode purposefully away down the track from their home. At the end of the track was a crossroads at which he turned right onto the pathway which ran in a near northerly direction. As he marched along he began to muse idly.

He knew he was tall for a mouse, and many of his fellow mice had suggested that a touch of water rat lay in his ancestory. He often wondered himself as to the truth of this, and would not have been surprised if it were so, especially as he had always had an affinity with rivers and had even swum in the sea once. And that would explain too the ancient sword, which he knew was a mariner's cutlass, as well as his liking for fishing.

'Oh well,' he thought, 'I suppose I'll never know for sure!' and turned his thoughts to the journey which lay before him.

He knew that the path ahead of him would soon peter out, and from then on he would need to follow the wide river to the City.

After a while Father Ticklemouse came to the end of the made up path and took a track up a lightly wooded hillside. He was aware from his fishing expeditions that, a short distance from the top of the hill, the track eventually led down to a tree-lined riverbank. From here he could follow the river upstream for the first part of his journey.

Although it was still relatively early, he had already covered quite a distance, so he thought that, before resuming his journey, he might stop for a short break when he reached the riverside.

As he neared the brow of the hill he began to discern the sound of voices. The closer he got the clearer the voices became, until he could hear precisely what they were saying.

'Untie me you unspeakable baskets and I'll show you what for!' came the sound of a deep angry voice.

A screech of sarcastic laughter and howls of derision greeted the outburst, as Father Ticklemouse carefully rounded the crest of the hill at a low crouch. The hairs on the back of his neck began to rise at the sight that lay below. As a precaution, he dropped quietly to the ground between some lemon grass fronds to conceal his presence.

In a glade close to the river, flanked by trees, stood four late adolescent weasels in various states of mirth. The object of their mockery sat beneath a large old oak tree, restrained by a dozen turns of strong sea rope coiled around the gnarled trunk. It was an adult male sea otter with a full flowing moustache, pierced ear and militia mariner's rig.

Even at the not inconsiderable distance from Father Ticklemouse's vantage point, the otter looked large, and though he appeared to

be tightly secured, the weasels made sure to keep well out of range of his thrashing tail.

'We'll let you go right enough, Fatso,' said the biggest weasel, who appeared to be in charge. 'Just as soon as the Raiders arrive. Then we'll see how tough you are!' he continued.

Father Ticklemouse hadn't seen weasels in this area for a long time and wondered what would bring slimy characters like them this far away from their normal territory. Also he didn't like the sound of 'Raiders', whatever they were, so he decided that he would do what he could to help the imprisoned otter.

Father Ticklemouse thought that due both to its size and its current aggressive state, the otter could probably have despatched four fully grown weasels single-handedly, let alone the juveniles who were taunting him. However, he was also of the opinion that it would be best if he could somehow release the otter from the bonds that secured him to the tree, without making his captors aware.

Indeed he wondered how the young weasels had managed to capture such a formidable creature, and guessed, correctly as it turned out later, that the animal had been sound asleep under the tree.

To free the otter, he would need to get round the weasels unseen, position himself behind the captive animal and, either cut through, or undo the knotted ropes. As gently and as soundlessly as he could, he withdrew his cutlass from its scabbard, clenched it between his strong white teeth, and began to slither down the hill towards the river and the back of the oak tree.

In a short time he had managed to reach the riverbank and from there he dropped silently to the water's edge. Now, completely shielded from view, he could make his way to a point directly behind the oak tree; and use its great size to continue obscuring the weasels' view of him.

When he had reached that position, Father Ticklemouse slowly eased himself up onto the bank and within a few short seconds had reached the back of the tree. All that remained to do now was attract the otter's attention to let him know what it was he planned to do. However, he knew that this would be easier said than done!

With his back to the tree he began carefully to edge around it, in order to get closer to the otter.

Emitting as loud a whisper as he dared, he said as he neared the animal,

'Psstt! Oi, Mr Otter!'

'What's that?' asked the otter.

'Sshh! I'm a friend, and I'm here to help, so keep it down,' said Father Ticklemouse, as quietly as he could.

'What's what?' asked one of the weasels, 'what are you goin' on about you great pudding? You goin' barmy or somefink.'

'I'll show you who's barmy, when I get out of this,' said the otter under his breath.

In the meantime Father Ticklemouse had started work on the knots. Fortunately they weren't too difficult to untie, so he didn't have to sever them with his cutlass.

He was glad of this, as he felt sure that the rope would come in handy in the future.

Crawling back round to the otter he said,

'Listen to me and please try to keep quiet. I've undone the knots so you just need to gradually slip the coils and get ready to run.'

'Run??!!,' said the otter contemptuously, trying to constrain his angry voice to a whisper, as he attempted to wriggle free, 'the last thing I'm going to do is run!'

And with that said and one last shrug he was up and out of the ropes, launching himself at the largest of the weasels in venomous fury. Father Ticklemouse was amazed at the speed with which one so bulky could move, and watched fascinated.

The first weasel sank to the ground, as if pole-axed; the result of being on the receiving end of a blow from one of the otter's ham-like fists. The remaining weasels, who had been lying on the ground recovering from their bouts of laughter, soon leapt to fighting positions and began to circle the otter, snarling and spitting. Suddenly the otter

17

leapt straight up in the air and in a single whirling movement battered the three remaining weasels with his thick tail. Each one suffered his leader's fate and soon the four ruffians lay unconscious on the grassy floor.

The otter stood surveying his work with his clenched paws on his hips and an air of smug satisfaction about him.

'Yes, um, well... showed 'em a thing or two. Might think twice before they go attackin' innocent folk while they're havin' a peaceful nap and minding their own business,' he said to himself.

'Now, what to do?' he went on. 'Can't leave 'em here, they'll just cause more trouble when they wake up.'

'I know,' he muttered, as if a good idea had suddenly occurred to him, 'that'll be just the job'.

Bending low the otter picked a weasel up under each of his burly arms and strode to the river's edge. As he did so, Father

Ticklemouse noticed a small rowing boat tied up next to a larger craft. The otter carefully and almost gently placed the two weasels in the boat, and then repeated the process with the remaining two. He then put the oars quietly next to the unconscious animals, untied the boat and gave it a shove out into the gentle current of the river.

With his back to Father Ticklemouse, who had by this time approached the otter, he grunted in a satisfied way, as if admiring his handiwork, while the boat moved slowly downstream.

'Err hmm, excuse me Mr Otter,' coughed Father Ticklemouse,

'Why bless me yes,' said the otter, 'Forgettin' my manners governor. Allow me to present the thanks of Timmo de Beauclet for your assistance,' extending one of his colossal paws and bowing as he continued, 'To whom might I be addressin' myself?'

'They call me Jethro' responded Father Ticklemouse as his own paw was enveloped by that of Timmo and shaken vigorously.

'Well Jethro, I have to admit I was in a right old pickle there. I dread to think what would have happened if you hadn't come along.'

'Glad to be of service, er Timmo,' responded Father Ticklemouse, 'Just one thing though, who or what exactly are Raiders?'

Chapter 3

Timmo's Story

'Ah, Raiders? So you want to know about the Raiders?' asked Timmo becoming more serious. 'Well now my dear guv'nor, I see you've got an old travelling sea stove with you, so why don't you make us a brew and I'll tell you what I know about those vermin.'

'A tale for a cup of tea is it? Sounds fair to me,' said Jethro setting up the stove. 'I'll just gather a little dried wood and kindling and strike a spark from my flint to get it started.'

Within a few minutes, the stove was roaring and Jethro placed a water filled kettle on top. While he waited for the water to boil he took a few leaves from a parchment folder and placed them in the two tin cups he had brought with him. As soon as the water was boiling he poured some into each cup, and waited while it brewed. Then, from a skin pouch he added some milk, freshly drawn earlier that day.

Finally he sprinkled into each, a little home grown beet sugar to sweeten the beverage.

Handing one mug to Timmo, and taking a swig from the other he looked at the sea otter and raised a quizzical eyebrow. 'Well?' he enquired.

'It might be best if I start by telling you about myself and where I hail from,' began Timmo.

'You can probably guess by the way I speak, that I'm from the southern lands. Come from a long line of sea faring otters and, like my forefathers before me, I've sailed all eighteen seas of the charted world. After years of adventurin' and generally seeking my fortune, I finally saved enough to return home to my village, buy a little fishing boat and settle down.

'I met and married a sparky teacher girl called Linith from Mersia,' he went on, 'and eventually we had two pups, Sofrah and Samwell.

Life was unadventurous, some might say boring, but it suited me down to the ground after all my shenanigans around the world.

My fishing boat and Linith's teaching kept us comfy with plenty to eat and things were goin' well until six quarter moons ago.'

'Why, what happened?' asked Jethro.

'The worst possible thing that can happen to a creature,' he replied quietly.

'Early one morning while I was out on the ebb tide away in Felday *Cove* after a shoal of flatties, 'they' sailed into the village, 'they' being the Raiders.

'They sacked the homesteads and laid waste to everything. They took some of the wives and children, the rest of the villagers they slaughtered,' he hesitated and choked on a sob.

'I got back an hour or two after they'd sailed off with most of the village's stores and provisions. Found my Sofrah dying by the entrance to our lodge,' he said.

Jethro's whiskers twitched as he listened. He could sense the emotion building in Timmo.

Much as animals today are in tune with unspoken feelings, he felt a surge of sympathy rise within him, as he imagined what it would be like to lose his own family.

'Look,' he said in a kindly voice, 'if you don't want to go on we can talk about it another time.'

'No guv'nor,' said Timmo, wiping the suggestion of a tear from his eyes. 'Best I carry on, then you'll understand what kind of beasts you're asking about and what, eventually, we'll all be up against.

'As I say I found my poor little darlin', pikestaff in hand, to one side of the entrance. She was the elder of the two, took after me she did, always up for a fight or a bit of sport, so much so that I'd been training her in the ways of the marine militia. I just didn't train her well enough, though.

'With her dying breath she told me what had happened. "Pa," she says "there were too many of them and they took Ma and young Sam.

24

I heard them say they were headed north through the inland waterways." Then she says, "Pa, I love you and Ma". And that was it, she died in my arms. My little girl, passed on to the Great Spirit.

'It was then that I noticed the dead bodies of two creatures, the like of which I'd never laid eyes upon before. Strange looking they were, with almost furless skin, but for some tufts of fine hair sprouting from their heads and bodies, which were mostly covered with studded leather jerkins and breeches. They had short, stout, strong looking legs, but their arms, which were just as muscular, looked out of proportion as if, because they were so long, they would drag along the ground.

'I'd like to think that she must have done for those two Raiders before being overwhelmed by the greater numbers of the rest of them.

'I spent most of the next day and a half working like a loonie, constructing a burial lodge for my daughter and the rest of the dead villagers.

'As for the dead Raiders I stripped them of their clothes and weapons and built a big fire. No more than they deserved.

'I stowed their kit on my small boat, grabbed Sam's pet pigeon and set out after them.

'Been following them for six quarter moons now.... following their trail of destruction. They seem to be taking a zigzag path northwards.

'I've sailed pretty much day and night since then, heaving to at bank side and comin' ashore for a bit of kip when I can go on no longer. That's what I was doing when those skulking n'er do wells roped me up. It was lucky for me that you happened along.'

Jethro was thoughtful for a while before speaking then he said, 'Look Timmo, it occurs to me that, as we seem to be headed in the same general direction, we might as well travel together, at least until we arrive at where we're bound or need to go our separate ways. What d'you think?'

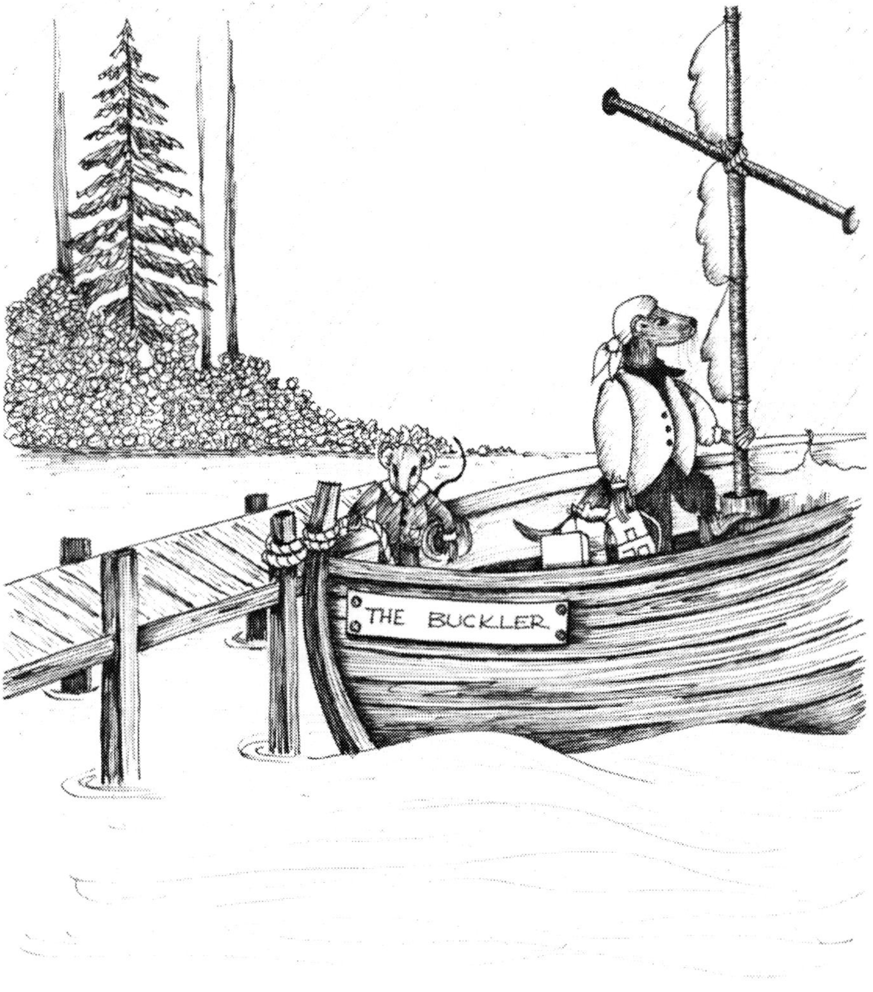
THE BUCKLER

'Sounds like a champion idea to me guv'nor,' replied Timmo. 'After all they say you're safer travelling in numbers than alone,' he continued, little knowing how sorely this notion would be tested later that day.

'I suggest we stow your tack on my boat and start out immediately,' he said, 'We've got the whole afternoon to make way, so we should be able to sail a fair way upriver before nightfall.'

Chapter 4

'Cat Attack'

After they had loaded all of Jethro's baggage on board Timmo's boat, Jethro noticed from the brightly painted name on each side of the front, that it was called *The Buckler out of Felday*. He moved to the rear, as Timmo beckoned him to sit down on a bench behind the small 'ship's' wheel.

'Alright,' Timmo said, 'as we're goin' to be shipmates, best I teach you some basic seamanship, or rather in this case river-craft. That is unless you know some already.'

'Well I'm a good swimmer for a mouse, but that aside, my knowledge is pretty limited' replied Jethro.

'Right then,' said Timmo, 'First off the front of the boat is called the bow and the back of the boat the stern. The bow is forward or *fore* and the stern is *aft*. The boat is tied off fore by a *bowline* and aft by a *stern line* when we're in dock or at bank side, and by an anchor when we're at sea.

'The right side of the boat looking forward is called *starboard* and the left side *port*.'

'When we 'set sail',' he went on, 'we unfurl and let wind into the sails, in order to move the boat. Once we're movin' we *trim* the sails to get the right balance of wind and movement, by adjusting the *sheets* which are the ropes attached to the bottom corners of a sail.'

'The ship's wheel controls the rudder which lets us change the direction of the boat. Then there's *tacking* ...'

'Hold up Timmo, there's only so much a mouse can take on board,' interrupted Jethro, 'No pun intended.'

'I suppose you've got a point guv'nor, maybe the best way to show you the ropes is by learning as we sail,' responded Timmo. 'So, I'll just cast off fore and aft, and we'll hoist sail and be on our way.'

Soon the small boat pulled out into the current and, with the ship's wheel in one hand and the sail sheet ends in the other, Timmo headed north a strong following breeze, which had just sprung up, at his back. For the next few hours Timmo alternated between barking instructions at Jethro and giving him words of encouragement, as Jethro slowly but surely got the hang of sailing the boat.

'My word guv you've certainly cottoned on quickly,' said Timmo, 'Here take a turn at the wheel on your own and let's see what you can do.'

The animals quickly changed positions and, as Jethro became more confident at handling the boat, he began to relax.

'Fancy a pipe?' asked Timmo, 'The weathers fair and what with you doing so well and all, I think you should be able to cope.'

'Why not?' replied Jethro.

Timmo handed Jethro a curly briar pipe and lit the contents using a clear piece of stone. A short clay pipe with the bowl moulded into a sea griffin's head soon appeared in Timmo's mouth and the stone quickly had that emitting small plumes of smoke as Timmo puffed away.

'What's that?' asked Jethro, 'Don't you need a flint and tinder? How does it work?'

'Well Jethro, this is one of the bits of kit I took from the dead Raiders. I found out by accident when I nearly set fire to myself with it.

'Fell asleep I did while I was looking at it. It was a sunny afternoon and I'd pulled in for one of my 'short' rests.

'It seems to work by concentrating the sun's rays into a point that's hot enough to ignite or burn anything combustible. Anyway it works well with a pipe providing there's enough sun out, which fortunately there is today.

'So,' continued Timmo, 'what about you? Where do you come from and what's your background?'

'Oh me?' replied Jethro, 'Well I'm quite a simple soul really, although my life has had its interesting moments.

'Basically I'm a country animal. Put me in the city and I can't stand it, I need the fresh country air, the smell of the flowers and vegetables from our garden, and the sound of the evening breeze rushing through my maize and barley crop.

'Besides I always seemed to get into trouble in the city, must be my country dweller's attitude, or my accent or something.

'My wife Hanna and I have got this small holding. About half a day's march from where you and I first met, close to a small village called Feldemore. We're pretty much self sufficient for food and firewood.

'What we don't have, we barter for with the locals and sometimes we take in travellers for lodgings, which also provides us with a little gold, or silver and sometimes even the odd small gemstone.

'As for my trip, well I'm off to collect my Hanna's grandmother from up north and bring her back to spend the winter with us. Even though we get frost and snow down here too, it's still a lot less cold than up there.

'Oh yes,' he said as if he had only just remembered, 'Hanna and I have got two fine youngsters, Gem and Ash. A right handful they are, I don't mind telling you, but they're worth it.'

He stopped as he realised that the happy picture that he had just painted was in stark contrast to Timmo's own situation, and might upset him. So changing the subject as subtly as he could he finished by saying:

'Anyway that's enough about me. I've finished my pipe now, so how about explaining 'tacking' to me?'

'Good idea,' replied Timmo.

For the next few hours they sailed up the river, until they noticed the shadows of the trees on the banks lengthening.

'Heave to, guv,' said Timmo, so Jethro began to steer the craft towards the starboard side bank. They approached the place that Timmo had pointed to, which looked a promising spot for a camp, as it was in an open clearing surrounded by bushes and trees.

Timmo leapt ashore with the stern line in one

of his great paws and tied it off around a convenient tree trunk.

'Let's have the bowline, please guv!' he bellowed to Jethro.

Jethro duly obliged and, shortly after, the boat was moored securely at both ends. The two animals then began unloading what they would need for that night's camp. Once the camp was set up, they had to collect kindling and cord wood in order to make a fire.

As Timmo explained, the fire would serve two purposes. Firstly they could cook their supper over it. This was to be a stew of onions and coriander, thickened with herb potato stock and topped by melted cheese and toasted bread.

Secondly, by taking turns at sleeping they could maintain the fire and keep away any predators lurking in the surrounding darkness.

Just before the sun's rays disappeared, Timmo had used the 'sunstone', as they had dubbed it, to set the kindling of dry leaves and grasses alight. He quickly added some small twigs and, as the whole began to blaze with yellow and orange flames, he gradually added larger and larger pieces of cord wood.

By the time darkness had fallen, there was a cosy fire roaring in the centre of the clearing. Jethro then removed a small cauldron and some short poles of metal and smoke hardened wood from his haversack. Soon he had fashioned a tripod from the poles and some binding cord, which would support the pot over the flames. Next he took the cauldron to the river and, bending low over the surface, swung the container down and filled it with water. Returning to the fire he positioned the tripod close enough to suspend the cauldron out over the flames.

Once the water was bubbling and boiling nicely away he started to add the various ingredients, which he left to cook until everything was soft and the stew was emitting a mouth watering aroma.

'Grub's up!' he shouted to Timmo, who had been cleaning and sharpening his sword, and checking various bits of his kit.

The two animals took their tin dishes to the simmering pot and Jethro filled each one in turn with a good helping. Sitting side by side in front of the fire they began to eat the delicious stew. Outside the natural bushy barrier, nothing appeared to stir.

Unless you were a Cat yourself, you could not have heard the stealthy padding of two large creatures prowling around the camp. The Cats were seeking a way in, but were discouraged from doing so by the heat and colour from the campfire, which even they could feel from where they were.

Inside the camp, Jethro and Timmo had finished their supper and were preparing for the night ahead. They had drawn straws to decide who would sleep for the first two hours and who would watch.

The result was that Timmo was to be the first to sleep, and Jethro would stand first watch.

Timmo curled up in front of the fire and was soon fast asleep.

Jethro sat, his back to the fire, looking out towards the surrounding woods. In this way he knew that he could feel if the fire were dying and add some more wood as necessary, whilst still being able to keep an eye out for intruders.

With his cutlass across his legs, he tried to position himself comfortably. He was very tired, having started early, and having experienced what for him was a very unusual and exciting day, what with the weasel incident, meeting Timmo and learning to sail.

Now animals have their own internal clocks and in ancient times, animals being more intelligent than nowadays, these biological clocks were much more sensitive to changes in behaviour. So it was that, as Jethro stared out into the darkness with only the low sound of Timmo's rhythmic snoring for company, he found it more and more difficult to keep his eyes open. Slowly his eyelids began to droop,

'Just a few ticks, won't hurt,' he thought, as he rolled over onto his back and fell fast asleep against the sleeping form of Timmo.

39

Only the glow of the fire illuminated the small clearing, but outside the Cats saw everything.

As the flames flickered lower, the fire died down to first gold, then orange, and finally red embers and the Cats began to move towards the clearing. The encircling bushes and shrubs were no barrier to them, as they leapt over and were inside the clearing, advancing slowly towards the sleeping animals.

Chapter 5

'How Jethro became a 'Ticklemouse''

The wind was warm and comforting on his face, almost hypnotic. Jethro smiled contentedly as he began to wake, but it was not the wind on his face, and there was nothing to smile about as he opened his eyes.

Towering over him and snarling, stood a huge Cat, a large forepaw on either side of Jethro. Magically the creature seemed to be growing bigger and bigger, until finally it had trebled in size.

'Timmo!' shouted Jethro in alarm, as he scrambled for his cutlass, 'Wake up! Quickly!'

For a moment, he had the sword, but with one swipe from the Cat's vicious claws it was knocked from his grasp, and he vaguely heard the distant clattering sound, as it struck the trunk of some nearby tree and fell to the ground.

Behind came the terrible sounds of Timmo and the other Cat locked in mortal combat.

Jethro knew their situation was hopeless, and mentally began to prepare himself for the worst. Animals in distress, even today, often enter a dream-like state, where they seem removed from reality. Jethro was no different. His mind began to drift as the immense weight of the Cat pinned his body to the ground, crushing the breath from him. Its paws, talons extended, moved slowly towards his throat. In a ghastly whisper the Cat spoke.

'Now you are mine, little mouse. My sister is dealing with your companion, just as I shall deal with you.'

But Jethro was far away. In his mind's eye, he was there again in Ash's room on his back, his two children lying on top of him. Slowly, as he had done then, he began to gently move his paws in the same fluttering motion. From a distance he thought he heard the sound of laughter, but it was not that of his son and daughter. It was a cold shriek, almost a whispered laugh, which soon developed into a low regular purring. Gradually, he felt the Cat relax, and, coming to his senses, he realised that, just as with his children, he might be able to mesmerise the Cat and control it.

'Get off me!' he commanded the Cat. To his amazement the Cat did just as it was ordered, and rolled away, saying, 'Yes Master', as it did so.

The sound of Timmo's struggle with the second Cat suddenly ceased, and there was silence except for Timmo's assailant, who began to speak.

'With your thrashing tail, and flailing fists, you have caused me pain, oh plump one. But now you shall pay for it with your life.'

At those words, Jethro's mind raced. What could he do? 'There must be a some way,' he thought to himself, 'perhaps if I.., that's it!'

Summoning up a strong confident voice he said to the now docile Cat by his side:

'Stop your sister.'

He barely heard the 'Yes Master,' the first Cat emitted, as it leapt with blinding speed and agility towards the Cat attacking Timmo.

In a moment the scene was transformed. Where before there had been silence, now the clearing was filled with snarling and spitting as the two Cats fought. Fortunately, the Cat under Jethro's control was larger, stronger and more ferocious than the one that had been about to kill Timmo, and it soon began to gain the upper hand. Jethro could hear Timmo's soft groans, but was unable to get to him as the Cats were in the way.

Without really thinking of the risk to himself, Jethro waited for the moment when he might position himself between the two Cats. Such an opportunity soon arose and he bravely wriggled under the belly of his Cat, who was now firmly on top of the other. Once in position he began the fluttering tickling motion over the lower animal's stomach and chest.

As he felt the vanquished Cat cease its struggles, he ordered the other to stand away, and continued stroking.

As with the first Cat, he soon heard the strange laugh of the beast beneath him, which died away to a low purring. Slowly standing up, and moving away, he spoke, 'On your feet, Cat!' he ordered in the same confident and commanding voice as before.

'Now, both of you stand back and stay still.'

'Yes Master,' they replied in unison, 'What ever you say Master.'

Jethro was now able to reach Timmo's side, and winced as he saw his companion's state. There was blood on the floor of the clearing and it wasn't the Cats'.

Kneeling down, Jethro carefully and tenderly examined the animal's wounds.

Timmo had deep wheals in his tail from where the cat had partially defended itself from the whirling and thrashing of Timmo's favoured weapon. There were cuff marks and bruising around Timmo's head, and the signs of bites to his shoulder.

Jethro knew that it was important to clean the wounds as soon as possible to stop any

46

infection, as this was ultimately more likely to cause death than anything else. He also needed to get Timmo warm in order to avoid shock setting in, as this too was dangerous. Many animals died from shock, particularly when subject to a vicious and unexpected assault.

Jethro was aware that the water from the river could be used to clean and bathe the wounds. However, he also knew that raw water might not be the best to use in this case. There could be substances in it which, although not normally harmful to animals, might react badly when used for this purpose.

A high priority, therefore, was to rebuild the fire, but not before he fetched their blankets and carefully laid them over Timmo.

The fire would have to be rebuilt next to the otter. Jethro knew it was too dangerous to move the animal to the remains of the old fire, even if he could, which he doubted, given Timmo's large bulk.

The other problem was that it was still the middle of the night and he was none too keen to move beyond their clearing in search of kindling. Fortunately they had collected plenty of cord wood and Jethro decided to cut some into shavings and thin pieces to get a new fire going. First of course he would need his cutlass, which he went in search of.

After a minute or two, he found it lying at the bottom of a tree trunk, where it had been thrown when the Cat had knocked it from his grasp. As he picked it up he noticed something. At its base, part of the metal handle, an ornate decorative mouse-head, which helped to keep a grip on the sword, was missing.

A few feet from the sword he found it, and as he picked it up, he noticed something unusual. The mouse-head consisted of a shaped brass sphere attached to a tubular section, which was pushed into the handle and twisted to secure it. The tube, which was hollow, had a rolled up piece of parchment partly protruding from it.

'I wonder what this is?' thought Jethro, removing the parchment from the tube and putting it into his breeches pocket, before refitting the brass mouse-head to the sword.

Putting thoughts of the parchment to one side, Jethro carefully moved the embers of the old fire to a position close to Timmo. Soon he had a respectable fire going to which he added the chopped up cord wood. He then fetched water from the river, boiled it up and when it had cooled, bathed and dressed Timmo's wounds.

His attention was distracted by the sounds of the Cats who, now returned to their normal size, were becoming more and more restless as dawn approached.

He moved to where they stood and spoke.

'Now Great Cats, by what names are you known?' he asked.

'Master,' said the larger of the two, 'I am Oarskar. My sister is Skowt.'

'Well Oarskar and Skowt, you are free to go, but remember that from this day forth I remain your master, and you will answer only to me! Now, leave!'

Yes Master,' they replied subserviently,

before leaping from the clearing and vanishing into the woods.

Jethro returned to where Timmo lay and was pleased to see that he appeared to have fallen into a deep peaceful slumber. It was then that Jethro remembered the rolled up parchment in his pocket. He took it out of his pocket and, sitting down, he unfurled it and, by the light of the camp fire, began to read. What he held in his paws would change his life, and those of whom he loved, for ever.

Chapter 6

'The Scroll of the Ticklemice'

Both sides of the scroll of parchment contained very small writing, which, to begin with, Jethro could not understand at all.

Jethro blinked as he peered and then slowly, the characters began to form themselves into recognisable words.

He began to read:

'The Scroll of the Ticklemice

Only he and he alone who is destined to understand these words will be able to do so. To all others they will be meaningless scribblings.

Read on then, if you can Stranger and discover your heritage, for you are a Ticklemouse. You are most likely the last of your kind, if events have fared badly for us.

Yours is a lineage that has run unbroken down from 10,000 cycles of the earth around the sun.

*In the beginning, the Great Spirit was abroad
and, for millennia upon millennia, all was well
with the creatures of the earth.*

*But then from the deep voids came the Dark
Spirit, a force which was as evil as the Great
Spirit was good.*

*For aeons the world stood variously under the
control of one or the other. At one moment the
Great Spirit held sway, the next, the Dark Spirit
prevailed.*

*That was until the Messenger arrived and, with
his follower, brought balance to the warring
factions.*

*With balance, the Dark Spirit and his forces
were banished to their own pocket of the
universe: an alternate world, where they held
permanent dominion.*

*On this world, the Great Spirit once more
reigned supreme, and peace returned.*

*Each world kept the other in balance: the
goodness of one world being counter balanced by
the evil of the other world. However, there was
one danger: it was prophesised that if ever one*

became stronger than the other, than chaos would follow.

With his work complete, the Messenger departed the world, but left his followers as guardians of the balance.

To begin with, there were eighteen, one for each of the eighteen seas. Each Guardian had his own talents or gifts of power, which could be used in the service of the balance.

Over the millennia that followed the balance was maintained but the eighteen became complacent; all except for one: the Ticklemouse.

The Ticklemouse was the least of the eighteen, but in spite of this, as the arrogance of the others caused each of their lines to falter and fail; it was the Ticklemouse line which stood strong.

The failing of the lines continued until only the Ticklemice remained as the last sons and daughters of the balance.

Only the Ticklemice and their descendants were left to maintain the balance by resisting the forces of the Dark Spirit.

Whoever you be, stranger, then know that you are a descendant of this line. You are a Ticklemouse, a last lost son or daughter of the Ticklemice.

As for your gifts of power, these may or may not have shown themselves already, but the passing of the true power only comes from the forefathers to the descendants.

Should the power not have been passed down to you for some reason, then Stranger, these last words will help complete what destiny has foretold for you.

Within the night, beyond your dreams,
Search for the light that no one sees.
To journey on before you sleep,
These words three times ye must repeat:

'Great Spirit, show your humble servant the ways of healing, the ways of defending and the ways of holding sway.'

With those last few words the writings on the scroll ended. Jethro emitted a low whistle, as the full importance of the words he had just read began to sink in.

He reached for the cutlass, and removing the tube, put the rolled up scroll inside it. He then reinserted the tube into the base of the cutlass, leaving only the brass mouse-head visible.

Day was dawning, and the warm bright sun coming up over the trees was welcome relief from the events of the night.

'Timmo,' remembered Jethro, 'I need to see how he's getting on.'

Jethro moved to the side of his companion, and was pleased to see the otter beginning to stir, although it has to be said somewhat weakly.

However, when Jethro bent closer, he could discern, to his dismay, small beads of perspiration on the creature's brow. Just then, Timmo opened his eyes.

But the look upon the otter's face was far from normal. He appeared to be staring madly, off into the far distance.

Then he started to speak, only not as he did normally. He spoke rapidly, but most of what he said sounded like gibberish. Jethro recognised the odd word like 'Linith, Sam and Sofrah', the last said in a desperate sad gasp.

Jethro realised that Timmo was in a delirious state due to a fever. He knew that this was nature's way of fighting off the infection, and that he could only sit by the animal's side and keep him comfortable.

Some hours passed, as Jethro alternately wiped Timmo's fevered brow and gave him sips of cold boiled water. However, Timmo was a tough character, and eventually the fever broke, and the otter awoke, back to some semblance of his normal self.

Hello mate,' he said weakly, 'I could murder a trout'.

'Right oh,' replied Jethro, 'but first I think we should put some distance between ourselves and this place. It's beginning to give me the creeps, and I don't fancy our spending another night here.'

Although he lost precious time in doing so, Jethro managed to pack everything up and load it onto *The Buckler*. Finally he helped Timmo struggle to his feet, and slowly they boarded the boat.

Once he had made Timmo as comfortable as possible, Jethro took up a position before the small ship's wheel, quickly hoisted the sail, and headed upriver.

Late in the afternoon, he spotted what he was looking for: a small tributary off the main river.

Heaving to, he tied up the boat, just at the junction of the tributary with the river. Soon he disembarked and, with a few words of reassurance to Timmo, slowly made his way up the stream.

Within a short while, the sound of the main river died away, and only the birdsong could be heard. Apart that was, from an occasional slurping, splashing sound in the water, upstream from where he stood.

Carefully and quietly he moved towards the water's edge, and waited and watched. Sure enough, he soon saw what he had expected. The 'slurping and splashing' sound was caused by several plump brown trout, rising from beneath the water to take the small flies that were floating down towards them every so often.

After a brief inspection of the flies that sailed, beyond the reach of the rising trout, towards him, he selected an artificial fly of about the same size and appearance from his fly box and tied it onto the leader on his line.

Now in fly fishing, unlike other kinds of rod fishing, there is no weight attached to the line. It is the weight of the thick fly line which flexes the rod and allows line to be worked out into the air, by false casting, before presenting the fly on the water. In order to deceive the fish a fine line or *leader* is attached to the end of the thick fly line, and then the fly is attached to this.

Beforehand, everything is greased up or oiled to make it slide easily through the guide rings on the rod, and float upon the surface of the water.

Jethro picked out the spot where the nearest trout was rising and cast the fly slightly upstream of the fish. As the fly floated back towards him, he retrieved some of the line in his left paw, so as to keep a reasonably tight line between the rod tip and the fly whilst being careful not to cause the fly to drag across the water's surface and put the trout off feeding.

Expectantly he watched and waited. After three casts, the trout gently sucked in his fly and, simultaneously raising the rod tip back and trapping the line between his paw and the rod, Jethro struck the hook home into the trout's bony mouth. He played the fish out, making sure to bully it away from its fellows, so as not to disturb them. Once on the bank, he despatched the fish swiftly, unhooked it and lay it on the grassy bank.

It glistened beautifully in the long shadowy sunlight, dark brownie black across its back with a creamy underbelly. Along its sides were black and red spots. Jethro silently thanked the Great Spirit as he always did when he caught his first fish.

Soon another equally plump fish joined its brother in Jethro's basket, followed by a third, and then he stopped fishing.

'One each for supper', he said to himself, 'and one for breakfast'.

He never took more than his immediate needs, knowing that this was the only way to maintain the valuable stocks of fish.

Back onboard the boat, he soon had his sea stove alight, and pan fried all three of the fish, saving the last one for their breakfast, the next morning.

Timmo, who was still a little weak, managed, albeit rather messily, to woof down his fish with more than a little relish.

After the meal, the two decided to move out into the river a little and anchor up before retiring to bed.

'No more Cats tonight!' they agreed.

Once Timmo was fast asleep, Jethro withdrew the tube from the base of the cutlass handle. By the light of a ship's lantern, he re-read the scroll of the Ticklemice. When Jethro reached the end, he thought to himself, 'Well, no time like the present'.

THE BUCKLER

Then, exactly as was instructed in the Scroll, he repeated the words of the incantation three times.

Immediately after he spoke the words, the lantern flickered and the space around him seemed to spin before his eyes.

After a while the spinning stopped and things slowed back down to normal, except that there before him, as if suspended in the air, stood the image of his long dead father.

'My beloved son,' said the spirit, 'the time seems long since my passing.

'I thought I would never see you again, and that this the moment of the passing of the ways would never take place.

'But thanks to the foresight of our ancestors, we may now begin the transference of these gifts of power and rebuild the guardianship of the balance.

'Jethro my son, you have already begun to learn, by chance, the way of holding sway, and as a result, you are now aware of the reason we are known as Ticklemice.

'Listen to me now and learn of the ways of healing and the ways of defending. Listen well my son for the fate of many will depend upon you.'

Jethro listened and, as the scroll had said he would, he went beyond his dreams and saw a warm white light beckoning him. Slowly he moved towards it, all the time hearing the kind and comforting voice of his father.

Chapter 7

'The City'

Jethro awoke the next morning as the sun's first rays broke over the hull of the boat and began to illuminate the space where he lay.

Rising into an upright position he stretched out as if to embrace the rapidly warming sunshine.

He remembered everything that had happened to him during the previous night, and he knew that he had changed. It was as if he had been subjected to several lifetimes' worth of teaching in one night.

His mind was positively bursting with knowledge, and from within the bubbling cauldron that was now his brain there rose unsummoned, the vision of a list of various herbs, tree bark, plants and roots.

He instinctively knew that this was to enable him to prepare a medicinal tea for Timmo which would speed the otter's recovery. So, weighing the anchor and unfurling the sail, he prepared to head for shore.

Once on dry ground Jethro moored the boat as gently and as quietly as he could, since Timmo was still asleep, and he didn't want to disturb him.

After a while Jethro had gathered all but one of the necessary ingredients for the medicinal tea, and made his way back to the moored boat.

When he reached it he heard a moaning sound, as Timmo began to stir.

'Feel as weak as a newborn cub, guv', he said as he sighted Jethro.

'Don't worry,' responded Jethro, deciding to take a chance and go ahead with preparing the medicinal brew, in spite of not having all the necessary ingredients, ' I'll soon have something ready to get you up and about.'

While he was preparing the medicine, he chatted to Timmo, who was munching on the remains of the leftover trout from the previous evening's meal.

'We must be fairly close to the City now Timmo. What do you reckon?' he enquired.

'There's some charts stowed under the bench seating in the stern, guv. Yes, those there, give 'em here if you please and I'll tell you in a jiff.' he replied.

'Oh yeah, and I'll need that pair of chart dividers too, for measuring.' he added.

After a few minutes, of measuring and scaling, he spoke.

'Well guv'nor, we're here,' he said pointing at a spot on the chart, 'an' the City's there.

'According to my reckoning, we should be there around midday, given a fair wind and a prompt start.'

'Sounds good to me,' said Jethro cheerfully, 'Just give me a few moments to change your dressings and clean you up. Then I'll get some of this medicine down you, and we'll be off, after we have breakfast.'

Soon the two were making good progress upriver and, while they sailed, Jethro related all of the events of the previous two nights to Timmo.

'My word, guv, or rather, should I say 'Master Ticklemouse'?' he joked, when Jethro had finished speaking.

'It's all a bit too much to take in. But if I've understood you correctly, you now have the power to mesmerise and control any animal, provided you can get close enough to *tickle* it.

'Also, you know ways of treating ailments and what the medicinal properties of roots, plants and trees are. Oh yeh, and what's that other thing? The ways of defending, tell me again. How does that work?'

'Well,' replied Jethro, 'to be honest, I'm not quite sure. After all, it was only last night, and I've not been in any kind of confrontation to test it yet.

'The best I can say is that it's a sort of non-aggressive style of fighting. Instead of striking blows at your opponent, you just block all his attacks on you, until he's exhausted and can't continue to fight.

'It's all to do with the *balance* that I was telling you about. You see, if someone comes at me all angry and worked up, and determined to do me harm, then I counter balance that by responding in a calm way and just absorbing their attack. That way the balance is maintained, and nobody really gets hurt.

'And I don't just use weapons for defence, like my cutlass or say a staff. My reflexes seem to have become much quicker.

'Look!' he said, and with a speed faster than the eye could perceive, he grabbed a fly which had been buzzing annoyingly around them for some time, and opened his paw to reveal it.

'By the great spirit, 'said an amazed Timmo, 'I've never seen anything like that before, or should I say 'not seen', as it was so incredibly fast.

'By the way, how should I address you now? Is Master Ticklemouse alright?'

'That sounds fine, but I think I prefer Jethro, and Guvnor's quite nice too. So why don't we keep it that way until we get used to what's happened to me?'

'Agreed, guv, mum's the word. Now I think I'll have a little snooze' he said breaking into a stretching yawn.

As Timmo had predicted, it was not long after noon that the little boat rounded a bend in the river, to reveal the City.

As Jethro steered the boat towards the shore, he noticed that the river seemed to make the shape of an elongated 'S'. The City lay along the straight line that joined the curved top and the bottom of the 'S'.

On the waterfront there had been constructed a wooden wharf, alongside of which boats of many sizes, styles and colours were tied up.

As he drew closer to shore, searching for a convenient place to moor up, Jethro even noticed an ocean going ship with multiple sails on each of its triple masts.

The dock was strangely quiet, with only a few rough looking animals, mostly weasels and sea frogs, going about their business.
Jethro guessed that, as it was around midday, many of the citizens would be eating their noontime meal.

Soon Jethro spotted a space large enough to tie up the 'Buckler', between one of the smaller 'big' ships and a coastal day trader, loaded with firewood and sacks of meal.

As he disembarked, leaving Timmo snoring softly in his slumber, Jethro approached one of the friendlier looking sea frogs, who was sweeping the deck on the adjacent ship, all the time whistling a merry shanty in a strange low croak.

'Excuse me sir?' asked Jethro.

The animal stopped the croaky whistling and sweeping simultaneously, and looked down at Jethro as if in surprise. He was gaily dressed in blue breeches and a blood red shirt, over which sat a pale leather waistcoat with no buttons. His head was adorned with a bright orange scarf, and, as he turned his head to look down, Jethro noticed a black patch over one eye. The other, uncovered and watery in appearance, peered down at the Ticklemouse, and the animal began to speak.

'Yes matey,' he said 'what can I be doin' for ee? And by the way I h'aint a h'officer so don't ee go addressin' me as *Sir*. My ship mates'll take the rise outta me, indeed they will. Most folk call me Patcheye.'

'Well Mr Patcheye,' said Jethro apologetically, 'my name's Jethro, and I'm looking for a doctor or an apothecary to get some herbs for my friend who's a bit unwell.'

'Well, 'ee be in luck my lad,' said Patcheye, 'Our ship's doctor is just avin' his lunch at the *River Rat Inn*, down the way.

'Fat old Toad he is, name of Wormold. Skip along there and I'm sure he'll sort 'ee out, but be careful it's a rough house, the *Rat*, and some nasty crew get in there. Tell 'im I sent 'ee.'

With that he gave Jethro directions for getting there, and they bade each other good day.

Jethro walked slowly along the wharf looking for the alley, at the end of which Patcheye had told him lay the *River Rat Inn*.

In a short while Jethro found what he was looking for and turned down a narrow dingy corridor between two buildings, made

71

gloomier by the fact that the sun's rays barely reached past the eaves of the overhanging roofs.

The inn was easily recognisable, as over the door, from a gallows bracket, hung a brightly coloured sign picturing a rat attired in riverboat gear at the rudder of a barge, smoking a clay pipe and looking ahead into the distance.

A little tremulously, Jethro opened the door and went in. He was greeted by a wall of sound consisting of chattering, much of which was in foreign tongues, accompanied by raucous singing to a shanty played on a concertina, in the gnarled webbed paws of a one legged sea rat.

As narrow and dingy as the alley had been, the inside of the inn made up for it, by being wide and high, and, with the exception of some corners, was brightly lit by wooden chandeliers suspended from the rafters supporting the roof.

The ground floor was entirely fitted out in ship's oak, with matching tables and bench seating occupied by various dwellers of woodland and water.

A first floor gallery, overlooking the seating area below it, was reached by a central timber staircase at the rear of the inn. Jethro assumed that lodging rooms led off from the gallery.

The gallery was supported at intervals by sturdy posts, between which heavy curtains were suspended by rings from stout dowel poles, allowing the individuals at the seating beneath to discuss business in relative privacy.

As he entered, the hubbub of the inn's chattering customers and the music stopped for a moment, while everyone looked up to inspect the newcomer. On seeing that it was only a countryside mouse, most resumed their business and the clamour started up again.

Jethro approached the bar at the back of the inn, on the right of the gallery staircase. Behind the counter stood a rather large toad, wearing an apron and dusting off some wooden goblets.

'Excuse me Landlord,' he began.

'Yes, Squire, how may I be of service?' returned the innkeeper.

'A half of burdock please, and a little information,' he replied, 'I'm looking for a Doctor Wormold.'

'Doctor?' said the innkeeper in an ironic tone, 'I've never heard him called that before, Squire! 'Sawbones' or 'Quack', yes, but never 'Doctor'.

'Anyway, 'Doctor' Wormold is right over there sitting at the table just by that large curtained off area.'

'Thanks Landlord,' said Jethro picking up his brimming mug and heading over to where the doctor sat, eagerly consuming his second helping of fried insects and pond weed.

Jethro stood by the table and coughed lightly to catch the animal's attention.

'Yes?' enquired the toad leaning back in his seat and lowering his spoon for a moment.

74

'The innkeeper told me you're Mr Wormold.' he began. 'I understand from one of your shipmates, a Mr Patcheye, that you might be able to help me. May I sit down?'

'At your pleasure m' dear sir', replied the other.

As Jethro sat down on the bench opposite Wormold, he noticed nearby, a large, dimly lit, curtained off section under one of the galleries.

For a moment, he thought he saw the curtains ruffle, but dismissing it from his mind as a trick of the light, he began to tell the good doctor why he wanted to see him.

'You see I'm in need of some Starwort leaves, for a medicinal brew. My companion and I, a sea otter named Timmo, ran into a spot of bother two nights ago with some Cats.

'Fortunately, we were able to escape, but Timmo was wounded and I was able to find everything I needed except the Starwort.'

'Well, by good fortune I happen to have some aboard our ship,' replied Wormold, 'If you care to wait while I finish my meal, I'll settle up and we'll be off.

'By the way, it's unusual even for a country dweller like your self to know of the medicinal properties of Starwort. How did you come to hear of it?'

'Oh, just an old family recipe handed down over the years' replied Jethro, judging it best not to go into any more detail.

'Yes,' he continued, thinking to change the subject, 'it's been quite an exciting few days I've had for a plain old country animal.'

He then related to the Doctor his first encounter with Timmo and the young weasels.

Just as he got to the part where Timmo had commenced setting about his adversaries, the curtain behind Wormold, was roughly drawn back to reveal not only the young weasels themselves, but also a group of large adults, all together occupying about two dozen places at their bench.

The brawny arm that had opened the curtain was connected to an equally brawny body, topped by an extremely gruesome head. The jaws in the head opened and began to speak.

'So there is a Dark Lord,' it began in an almost whispered sneer, before continuing on, the voice rising to an angry rant.

'You must be the little coward that sneaked up on my boys and let that mad animal loose on 'em, and now you're going to pay for it. Get 'im lads! Let's tear 'im to pieces!'

No sooner did the words drop from his cruel lips, than the weasel leader, for that was what he was, launched himself at Jethro, snarling and screaming, swiftly followed by his fellows.

Without being aware of how he did it, Jethro sprang back, upwards and out of his seat, and, landing adroitly, stood ready in the central open area of the inn facing the oncoming weasels.

He had never felt so calm and focused in his life. To his surprise, he felt not the least fear, though he knew he was vastly outnumbered.

The leading weasel made to slash open Jethro's face, but his claws fell on empty air, as Jethro swiftly stepped to one side and lightly touched the side of his assailant's upper arm diverting it to one side, and causing the blow to miss its mark.

The world stayed at normal speed for all but Jethro. His assailants seemed to be moving in at a very slow pace towards him, as he blocked and parried their blows at enormous speed.

Finally, he was beginning to wear them down, when, to his dismay, more curtains started to open, as the other customers in the inn became aware of the commotion.

Some of the drapes, when fully drawn back, revealed more bands of weasels rising angrily from their seats to join their fellows in the attack on him.

Unused as he was to his new abilities, Jethro realised that he might eventually be overwhelmed.

As if to bear this out, he found himself slowly but surely being forced back into a corner, far from the entrance. Jethro redoubled his efforts, but more and more weasels began to pile in, their blows beginning to strike home.

From the corner of his eye, he noticed the entrance door slowly opening, and felt an inward sense of relief, as a huge figure came bursting in,
all the while shouting, and thrashing about his tail.

'Guv'nor, Jethro, Master Ticklemouse, hold on mate I'm coming!'

Timmo's arrival was just what was needed to swing the balance back in Jethro's favour, and after several minutes the floor of the inn was strewn with broken furniture and weasels, either too exhausted to continue or laid out by Timmo's huge fists and thrashing tail.

'Thank the Great Spirit, Timmo,' said Jethro catching his breath, 'but I thought you were asleep in your sick bed?'

'Yes, er well, um, I woke up feeling great. That potion of yours seems to have worked

wonders, in spite of bein' missin' one of the ingredients.

'Thought I'd have a stroll about, when I ran into your new mate, Patcheye. Told me where you'd gone, he did. So I thought to myself, "do I feel like a bevvie with my good mate Jethro? Indeed I do!" Looks like I arrived just at the right time.

'Anyway, what have we here? I wonder?' continued Timmo, suddenly noticing the weasel leader lying on the floor and grabbing him by the scruff of the neck.

'What's your name ugly? And what are you doing around here?' he asked dragging the unfortunate weasel's head towards him.

The weasel's foul mouthed response only prompted Timmo to tighten his grip slightly so that he began to restrict the animal's breathing.

'I say again, who are you and what are you up to?'

This time the weasel was more polite, and
after begging in a wheezy croak for Timmo to
ease his grip, which he did, the weasel leader
began to speak.

'

Chapter 8

'Nevets Speaks'

'They calls me Nevets,' began the weasel chief grudgingly.

'An' I'm a chief of the Hibernian clan, as was my father before me and his afore him.

'Our camp is up north, and there we were minding our own business, just a bit of egg thievin' and bashing up locals who've got above their station, when a delegation comes to us from our cousins in the east.

'They says they wants to give us a message from the Raiders.

'Never 'eard of these Raiders before, but we soon began to find out all about 'em, and regretted it.

'I was ordered, ordered mind you, to attend a council with the Raider general and his officers. I don't take to bein' ordered about, especially in me own manor, as it were, but the look on our cousins' faces when I started flyin' off the 'andle, soon convinced me otherwise.

"'No Nevets," they pleaded, "you don't know what they're like, and what they can do. Their leader and his officers got fearful powers. Like sorcerers from kids' fairy tales and they've got our families. They're 'oldin 'em 'ostage, an' if you don' come..." Then their voices trailed off as if they couldn't bring themselves to talk about something too awful to even think about.

"'They'll what?" says I, but no matter how I bullied and badgered them, all's I got was more pleadin' and moanin' 'bout their families.

'Eventually, I gave in and went with 'em. Had to take along the oldest most useless one o' me tribe, at the Raider general's strict command.

'T'was a puzzle to me at the time, but I found out later when I met 'im, why he wanted someone, and what he wanted to show us.

'Anyways, eventually we arrives at their camp and gets to meet these 'ere Raider boys.

The first thing is they're like no animal nor beast I've ever seen before. Strange paws and feet, and that's without even considerin' their overall look, plus they give off an awful stink'

At this point, Timmo interjected:

'Yeah, we know what the baskets look like. Leastways I do, and Master Ticklemouse knows what I told him about 'em.'

'Timmo!' said Jethro through gritted teeth, 'Careful with the "Ticklemouse",' he pleaded.

'Oh yeah guv, sorry forgot myself I did,' he replied, 'Alright then Nevets, carry on now.'

'Well, shortly after arrivin' I gets introduced to their leader.' went on Nevets.

'As soon as he opens 'is mouth I begins to understand why my cousins bin agitatin' so much.

'His voice has the cold whip o' winter wind after the first snows and frosts. Cuts deep into you, makin' you feel like you gotta get away, but it's strangely fascinatin' and hypnotic too, like you can't leave 'cos your 'anging on his every word.

'"Weasel Chief," he says all sly and vicious like, "I am the General Legin, and you will do what I say."

'I could barely nod, as then he says, "Send hither the crone, I requested you bring!"

'At my word, the useless old article I'd brought walks over to General Legin.

'"Now", says he, "know the power of the Raiders and tremble. Kneel crone!"

'But she's hard of earin' and doesn't move quickly enough, so he raises his arm, and touching her head, he shouts "Down vermin!"

'Down she goes, but not because she's doin' anythin' of 'er own accord. It's like she's bein' transformed into some other kind of beast. In a few moments she goes from bein' perfectly upright to down on all fours. An' another thing, she looks like a young animal, a four legged one wi' no coverin's but her fur.

'When I asks her if she's alright, she just makes strange noises what I can't understand, and starts scurryin' about across the floor, like a brainless idiot.

'Then 'e speaks to me, "Weasel of the Hibernias, you have seen how great my powers are, and, unless you do as I say, then you and your kind will suffer the same fate as the crone. You will be doomed to spend a meaningless life, fit only for our nourishment and amusement, never more to take pleasure in your surroundings, nor to understand any but the most basic communication.

'"However, if you carry out my instructions well, I might, just might, let you and your family remain as you are"'

'Well I don' mind telling you I nearly pooped in me pants, shakin and shiverin' all over I was. Understood, now I did, why my cousins were so frightened.

'That trick of his though, not all the Raiders can do it, only him and the top officers, and by the way it don' seem to work on the Cats. I overheard two o' their foot soldiers, goin' on about havin' to bury one o' the bosses on account of him havin' tried it on with a Cat and comin' off second best.

'Anyway where was I? Yeah, then he tells me that they're the first wave of an invasion force. Crack militia, he said, and eventually, they're takin' over. He tells us we're to guide 'em through the country so that they can capture and make slaves o' the females and the young an' begin the destruction of our way of life.

'We were to go down south wi' em first, and then back up to the north east near to *Idloyes*, where they landed their small fleet of invasion boats. Then they'd ship out an' off back 'ome with their captives to plan the next phase of the invasion.

'Oh yeah, and they're intendin' on leavin' a small command post, to start makin' preparations for when they return with their main force.

'An' that's when you found us. We were coverin' the rear of the Raider's returning troops, and pickin' up any stragglers, as we followed on after them'

Timmo's grip on the weasel slackened, and he released the animal with a low whistle, as he took in the full significance of what they had just heard.

The weasel chief, sat down on a bench facing the entrance and rubbing his throat vigorously in attempt to relieve the soreness.

Before they could do anything, he made a sudden dash for the door and was gone. Timmo made as if to go after him, but Jethro's restraining arm held him back.

'Look, never mind him for now, I think we need to get back to the boat and head north as quickly as we can,' he said.

'Let's help the landlord tidy up, get some fresh supplies and be off. I need to get to Nana's as quickly as I can and make sure she's alright, and then I'll give you a hand to get your family back.'

Later that afternoon, *The Buckler* headed out into the wide river and turned onto a northerly course with all sails rigged to make way at the fastest possible speed. In the evening, when the wind dropped, the pair anchored up in mid-stream, made up their beds and drifted off into sleep.

In the morning they awoke early, washed and breakfasted, and then continued on their way.

Many miles north of them, in the tent of General Legin, Nevets, who had journeyed non-stop at great speed throughout the night, had just finished recounting what had happened in the City the afternoon before.

'And you say Nevets,' asked the General Legin, 'that the big one called his fellow companion Master Ticklemouse?'

'Yes my Lord,' returned the Weasel.

'How interesting, I thought their kind had been wiped out long ago. This explains something that's been puzzling me for some days now.

'That family of mice we captured, to the south west of here, the mother and the two young. They gave off a very faint, but familiar scent, one I have not sensed in ages.

'Bring them to me at once.'

A few moments later, the adult female and the two young stood frightened, but defiant, in front of the General Legin.

'Mistress Ticklemouse!' began General Legin,

'Tell me about your husband.'

'Ticklemouse? Ticklemouse? I don't know what you're talking about', she replied, and turning towards the two children, she asked,

'Do either of you two know what he's on about? Gem? Ash?'

'Don't worry,' came the chill voice of General Legin,

'You soon will know. You soon will, and when you do, you may live to regret the knowing of it. If you're extremely unfortunate, that is.'

Hanna clutched the two children to her, as if it would protect them. however, inwardly she felt a rush of fear surging through her body, as the blood ran cold in her veins.

Chapter 9 –

'The Way North'

Over the next few days the little boat, with the two animals taking turns at the helm, made good progress. Stopping only occasionally, to feed or take on water, and when the wind was too weak to power their sails, they eventually arrived in the country of the north, as most animals called it.

Jethro knew this because the surrounding land had begun to change. Where before there had been flat open fields and woodland, alternating with gently rolling hills, now in the distance there were more prominent and higher peaks. Some were round topped and others craggy like a group of sleeping giants watching over the mixture of brilliant green grassed and yellow gorse covered valleys below.

By straining his eyes, he could see that some of the mountain tops had the barest trace of snow. A sure sign, he knew, of the coming winter. As for the rest of the year, they were free of the beautiful yet potentially treacherous covering.

Soon, Jethro pointed towards the starboard side shore. 'That's it Timmo, that's where I need to get off. Then it's just about half a day's march to Nana's cottage.'

Timmo turned the boat towards the shore in the direction that Jethro had been pointing, and soon had the vessel moored up on a pebbly sand bank, which ran down from the gorse covered lower terraces of the northern mountains.

'Well my friend,' said Jethro, 'What will you do now?'

Timmo hesitated for a moment, and with a thoughtful look upon his face, he began to speak.

'Half a day's march there guv, half a day's march back with a night's rest in between, that's almost two days lost in regaining the trail of the Raiders,' he mused.

'Puts me in a bit of a quandary, so it does! First off we pretty much know where the Raiders will be headed. My guess is they'll go north east to the coast and their boats.

'That's beyond and to the seaward side of where this Nana of yours lives. So I could go with you as far as her house, rest up and then carry on in the hope of pickin' up their trail.

'As for you, you could bring her back to the boat, cut across the North East passage, I'll show you how on the charts, and join the river that starts in the mountains and runs down to the sea.

'Then you can meet me at *Idloyes*. That's the village on the coast, the one which the weasel chief mentioned.

'From the way our friend Nevets described the Raiders' landing point, I'd guess they're camped about a quarter of a day's march to the north of *Idloyes*.

'Only problem is we'll be deep in Cat territory, so we'll have to take care. You might be well advised to leave your old Nana on the boat.'

'I'm not sure she'll have that,' laughed Jethro, 'She's very independent and quite tough for her age.'

'Well, no matter,' said Timmo 'you just do the best you can.'

With that, they put together their kit, disembarked, and started on their way towards Nana's small village, the Hamlet of *Vale*.

They had not been journeying for very long before they rounded a narrow bend, and were met by a greatly agitated group of animals: males, females and young, rushing towards them from the opposite direction.

At the sight of Timmo and Jethro, the panicky band slowed to a trot. That was when the leading animals began shouting:

'Clear the path, Strangers. Make way the Raiders are coming. Flee for your lives!'

However, both Jethro and Timmo halted, blocking the path as they did so. Where they had stopped, the track narrowed down to pass between two rocky outcrops, and the oncoming animals were therefore also forced to stop.

'Now then my lads and lasses,' started Timmo, using all of his military bearing to create an air of authority, 'What's all this creatin' for?'

The leading animal, an ageing hare, spoke first.

'If it please you my lord, we were just escaping from the Raiders. We've been watching out for them for some time. Ever since we heard they'd landed at *Idloyes* two moons ago.

'A few days ago, one of our scouts realised that they were on their way by the dreadful racket they were making as they approached our village. Didn't seem to care who knew they were coming.

'Anyway, we got together as many of the community as we could and hid until they passed through. Unfortunately not all of us were able to find safe hiding places, and some were found and carried off by the Raiders. Chained up, they were, to the other poor animals that the Raiders had already captured.'

Jethro, who had been listening with a mixture of impatience and mounting concern, could no longer restrain himself,

'Do you know my wife's grandmother, Nana?' he asked.

'Er, yes,' responded the hare, reluctantly.

Sensing from the other's tone that all was not well, Jethro went on,

'She was one of those who was taken wasn't she?' he asked insistently.

'I'm afraid so, my lord,' replied the hare.

'I'm very sorry, but there was nothing we could do, they were terrible frightening creatures. All we could do was save ourselves.'

'I understand,' said Jethro, 'You don't need to reproach yourself. At least she's alive.'

'Did you notice which way they went?' he asked.

'Well, I can't be sure,' answered the Hare, 'but from what we were told previously when we first heard of them, I'd say they were headed back toward *Idloyes*.'

'One more thing you ought to know,' he went on, 'when they took Nana, we heard some shouting amongst the group of prisoners. A female and two youngsters started calling to her. "Nana over here," they said, "It's us, Hanna, Gem and Ash."'

As he heard the words, Jethro's heart froze, the icy grip of fear beginning to spread through him.

'And now good sir,' said the Hare interrupting Jethro's thoughts, 'if you'll forgive me, we must speed on. We're headed as far south as we can go. Anything we can do to put the utmost distance between those Raiders and ourselves.'

With that, Timmo and Jethro stood aside and the remnants of the inhabitants of the Hamlet of *Vale*, resumed their journey, headlong down the path.

'Timmo,' said Jethro aghast, 'Whatever can we do?

'They've both our families now,' he went on,

'We've got to find a way of catching them up, but the Raiders have such a good head start, and now the weather's beginning to turn as well.

'Timmo,' he went on agonisingly, 'have you the faintest idea of what we might do, because I fear I'm at a complete loss?'

'Well guv, as it goes, actually I have,' replied Timmo.

'First off, there's no point goin' on to *Vale* is there?

'Second, the Raiders, as you say, have got a head start on us, and even tho' they'll be slowed by their prisoners, there'd still be a considerable distance for us to make up.

'The danger is that, before we can catch up with them, they'll reach *Idloyes* and their boats, and then be off back to whatever spirit forsaken hole they crawled from.

'So I reckon our best chance is to get back to the boat as quickly as we can and take the north-east passage that I was telling you about.

'It won't be easy, and we don't know what obstacles we might have to face, but we've got to try it guv, or it's goodbye forever to all those whom we love and hold dear!'

Chapter 10 -

'The Chase Begins'

Jethro and Timmo made good progress on the way back to the boat. This was partly due to it being downhill, and partly because they knew the route a bit better, from their outward journey towards Nana's village.

When they arrived at the riverbank they leapt aboard *The Buckler* - having first untied the lines securing the boat - and immediately hoisted the sails.

Jethro stood at the small ship's wheel, a look of grim determination and resolve upon his face, whilst Timmo pulled out the charts and began seriously studying the route they would need to take.

'If we can make good time we'll be at the estuary before tomorrow's evening tide,' he said. 'I just hope we get there before they ship out.'

Just then, a look flickered across his face, as if he had suddenly remembered something extremely important.

'Of course why didn't I think of it before? What a fool I am!

'Jethro, heave to for a mo' and bring me the cage with Sam's pet bird in it. Now if you please!'

As Jethro handed him the cage, Timmo whipped off the sheet covering it and opened up the door.

'Here, hold her for me,' he said as he handed the bird to Jethro.

For a moment Jethro hesitated and inside himself he squirmed. He hadn't mentioned it to Timmo, but ever since he had been young, he'd had a phobia about birds, and normally couldn't stand to touch them. He felt the same old panic starting to rise. Then he remembered his family and their plight and knew that whatever it was that Timmo was up to, it must obviously be for the good of both of their families.

Inside his head, he seemed to hear the voice of his late father saying, 'You are a Ticklemouse Jethro. The last of a sacred and

104

noble line. Take courage from that and remember that you can always draw on the inner strength bequeathed to you by me and your ancestors. In that way, you will come to know that you need fear no creature: fowl, animal or homenim.'

With that, his fear seemed to evaporate and he grasped the bird, wondering all the time as he did who or what a 'homenim' could be.

'Right ho guv,' said Timmo, 'just give me a moment. I need to write something down and attach it to that thing's leg'.

Having hastily scribbled a note he placed the small piece of rolled up parchment into an equally small tube with leather straps. These he used to tie the tube onto the pigeon's leg, before gently releasing it into the air.

In the meantime, Jethro swiftly re-hoisted the sails and the small boat moved forward with increasing speed as the wind filled them.

Setting course in line with Timmo's instructions, Jethro looked ahead whilst keeping an ear open to listen to Timmo.

Then Timmo continued by saying, 'Right ho guv, let's make way as fast as we can. And by the by, just in case you're wondering what in the shades is goin' on, I'd better explain.'

'Y' see' said Timmo, 'when I was in the marine militia, me an' my fellow mariners, we were all the best of mates, and looked out for each other.'

'We had this tradition, we did, that if one of our number left the service and got into a spot of bother, he'd have a way of letting his shipmates know about it.'

'That way if the Militia weren't too far away, and weren't engaged in other more pressing business, they'd receive word and, as many as could, would come to their shipmate's aid.

'So when I finally left them to settle down, they gave me this bird. It's a carrier pigeon. No more plucky creature you could wish to meet. Never had to use her before, had no cause to. Samwell took to her as he grew and looked after her. We just kept her caged at night, and let her out every so often when she got broody or needed to stretch her wings.

'But now it's different kettle of ship's tea, as we used to say. And, although it's a slim chance, there *is* a chance that we can use her to contact my old shipmates. That might just make all the difference if they get the message in time.

'Anyway, best we concentrate on the job in hand. Now where did I put those charts?'

It was mid afternoon by the time they reached the junction of the two rivers at their source, the Delta Falls.

As they neared the Delta Falls they couldn't help but be amazed at the sight that met their eyes: one that had been seen by very few animals.

Rising up ahead of them stood a great waterfall, which tumbled down all of one hundred metres by modern-day measures.

Made up of rain water, and pure high mountain streams mixed with water from aquifers and underground rivers, it roared as it crashed and cascaded into a deep lagoon at the bottom.

At each end of the lagoon, just like two branches, the water flowed out as a newly created river. One branch ran down in the direction that Timmo and Jethro were coming from. The other was the head of the river that wound its way down towards the coast and eventually met the sea at *Idloyes Bay*, about a day's journey away by boat.

'Steady as she goes, guv'nor. It's goin' to be a bit tricky here,' warned Timmo, 'There's bound to be a few underwater rocks and boulders, and what with all this noise and churned up water where the waterfall hits the lagoon, there's a risk of doin ill to the boat.'

No sooner had the words left Timmo's mouth, than there came the sickening sound of timber against rock, as the boat groaned and one side of it fractured.

'Jethro!' shouted Timmo above the clamour, 'Quickly, we've got to get her ashore to see what damage has been done. Head for that shingle beach over there!'

Jethro realised by their sluggish progress and the strange angle at which the craft sat on the lagoon, that they must be taking on water. Inwardly, he felt the beginnings of desperation seeping into his mind.

Eventually the prow of *The Buckler* slithered onto the shingle, and came to a halt. The two animals, under Timmo's direction, tied off the bowline to a nearby boulder, and then dragged the stern around by its line until the whole of the side of the boat was exposed to air.

As soon as they had tied off the stern, they rushed to look at the damaged hull. A gaping hole met their gaze, water flowing out onto the shingle, now that the boat was beached.

'She's goin' no further guv, that's for certain,' said Timmo.

'There's nothing for it,' responded Jethro, 'we'll just have to take the bare minimum we need and continue on foot.'

As they packed their essentials into two haversacks, both animals realised that their chances of success were disappearing as rapidly as the water was running out from the hole in their boat.

They had faced many trials together in their short association, and each decided not to let their concern show, but to put the best face on things as they could. However, Timmo expressed what worries they could express openly when he said,

'Guv, you know we're deep in Cat country, don't you?'

'Yes,' replied Jethro 'and that we're probably going to have to travel all through the night, if we've any chance of getting to the Raiders before they leave.'

'Still, look on the bright side Timmo,' he continued, 'I'm not the mouse I was when we first met.

'Without wishing to be boastful, I'm more now. A lot more, and don't forget we've got the experience of our previous run in with the Cats to help us. It's not exactly as if we're unaware of how formidable they are.

'We'll just have to stay close to each other and be vigilant,' he concluded.

'That, and quiet and careful, not to mention lucky,' Timmo added.

'One thing though,' said Jethro, 'always assuming we make it to the Raiders' encampment in time, they're not exactly going to welcome us with open arms, are they? In fact, we'll probably have trouble even getting past their guards.

'So I've been thinking. You've still got the kit from those two raiders have n't you?'

Timmo nodded and Jethro went on:

'Well then, let's dress me up in one of their sets of gear. I doubt, from how you described them, that any of their stuff will fit you, and, if needs be, I can pretend to be one of them who's captured you and is bringing you in.

'I suggest we take that sea rope the weasels had you tied up with when we first met each other, so that I can tie you up,' he went on, 'I expect with your mariner background you know a few trick knots that'd be easy to get out of?'

'Fair right you are there guv,' replied Timmo. 'I'll just get their gear and help you on with it. We might need to make a few adjustments for it to fit you, given what a misshapen bunch of baskets they are.'

At last Jethro was re-kitted out and, if not exactly like a Raider, would, in Timmo's opinion just about pass for one at a distance, and even more so at night time.

As the shadows lengthened the animals set off, going as swiftly as they could over the scree by the side of the river. Soon the ground began to fall away and, in an undulating fashion, opened out into a tree lined valley.

After covering some distance, and with sunset fast approaching, the path ahead of them began to rise again steeply. As they crested the brow of the hill, they saw in the hazy distance, the reflections of the late autumn sun glittering on the surface of the beautiful blue and emerald coloured ocean.

Chapter 11

'The Return of the Cats'

As they stood for a moment at the head of the slope, there stretched out in front of them a broad glade, which ran between the edges of the forest on either side.

The sun sank lower, as evening fell, and the beginnings of a chill breeze were felt by both animals.

'There's nothing for it guv,' began Timmo, 'you were right. We'll have to carry on marching through the night, if we've a spirit's chance of catching the Raiders!'

'I know,' agreed Jethro, 'and maybe now would be a good time to consider what we'll do if we run into any Cats.'

'In my opinion,' he went on, 'we should stay close to one side of the glade within touching distance of the woods. In that way, we'll be a little less obvious or visible to anything that wants to turn us into its supper.'

'Also,' Jethro added, 'if something does happen, I want you to use the rope to hoist yourself up into the nearest tree.'

Timmo, with a look of great disgruntlement on his face, started to disagree, but Jethro cut across him and continued,

'Look Timmo, no offence, I know you're pretty much of a handful when it comes to a fight with most creatures. And that you're worth at least a dozen weasels, but I don't want to risk your getting hurt again. Plus you might be a distraction to me while I'm trying to control the animals attacking us.'

'Alright guv, but there's one condition. You must let me do what I can to help you from the trees.

'I'm a bit of a dab hand with a rope and noose end. It comes of playing idle games during our spare time in the mariners.'

'I suppose I can live with that,' smiled Jethro in agreement, 'but only if you promise to be extremely careful.

'Remember, if anything happens to me, you'll be the only hope for my family, not to mention your own Linith and Samwell.'

By now the sun had set and an almost full moon rose into the night sky, illuminating the land below. The two animals fell into a steady march and, as silently as they could, made their way down the hillside towards the western boundary of the glade.

As they reached the edge of the glade, they heard the first distant howlings of the wild denizens of the wood.

Both animals stiffened, and they slowed instinctively to a stealthy walking pace. The look in their eyes, as they turned to face each other, spelled out their mutual concern in unspoken words.

As they continued on, the howling gradually increased in intensity, until suddenly it ceased altogether, and everything became silent and still.

Timmo and Jethro halted directly beneath a large tree and stood, for a few short moments, leaning against the huge trunk. In the dark shadows, they remained motionless, shaded by the overhanging branches from the bright moon in the chill night sky.

'I don't like the look of this,' whispered Jethro, 'I think you should get yourself up into this tree as quickly and as quietly as you can, Timmo.'

Reluctantly the otter uncoiled the rope and, after swinging the noose round above his head a few times, he launched it up and over the lowermost branch. He worked the loop down over the other side of the branch, until he could reach it and then pulled the plain end through the looped end until it was secured tightly against the bark of the branch.

Then, more deftly and acrobatically than Jethro would have imagined possible of him, Timmo hoisted himself up. He removed the rope from the first branch and retied it on to a slightly higher leafier one where he might stand concealed, but still able to view the ground below and its surrounding areas.

118

Slowly, so as not to draw attention to himself, he carefully drew himself up onto the branch, stood up and waited.

He had barely gained his vantage point, when he heard a low growling and mewling from below.

He watched in a mixture of dismay and amazement as fully a dozen huge Cats entered the glade from the woods on either side, in front of and behind where Jethro stood.

Jethro also remained transfixed as further Cats entered the glade, until around twenty of them, stood, raised tails moving from side to side, looking, for all the world, as if they were preparing to leap upon him. As with his previous encounter with Cats, they began to increase in size until, in awesome magnitude they glowered frighteningly under the chill night sky.

Jethro knew that the *Tickling* gift he had now was quite different compared with how it was before his father had spoken to him. It was more powerful and could be achieved

119

almost instantly. He knew that all he had to do to control an animal was to touch it on its forehead and project his commands by thought or words.

Even so, twenty Cats was a large number, and in spite of the great speed he now possessed, he knew that the Cats were considerably quick themselves; certainly faster than most other animals.

Rather than wait, Jethro decided that, as the saying goes in the marine militia, swift and surprise attack is the best form of defence.

With blinding speed he leapt towards the nearest Cat. Simultaneously touching it on the head and projecting a command of 'Come to my defence!' he then sprang on to the next closest Cat.

By the time the remaining Cats realised what was happening and began to counter attack, he had control of six out of the twenty, and was directing these to attack their uncontrolled fellows.

That made it six against six, leaving eight other Cats still uncontrolled and free to attack him. The odds were improving, but not quickly enough, for Jethro's liking.

From above, Timmo watched in frustration, and marvelled, as his friend, barely a blur, moved amongst the Cats.

He could also see that, in spite of the great strides Jethro was making, the reality was that the situation had only gone from absolutely impossible, to extremely unlikely, that Jethro would survive.

Quickly untying the rope, Timmo took hold of it between his huge paws and, waiting for his chance, hurled the noose-end of it, like a lasso, through the air above the heads of the two nearest uncontrolled Cats. With great skill and dexterity, he managed to close the noose over both their necks at the same time. Then using all his immense strength he dragged them off balance long enough to allow himself to lift them back up onto their hind quarters, tie off the rope end and thus restrain the raging beasts.

In the mean time, Jethro had managed to gain control over two more Cats, but only at he cost of expending a great deal of energy, both physical and mental.

His blocking manoeuvres and twists and turns prevented the Cats from wounding him, but they also hampered him in his attempts to place the beasts under his control.

He was really beginning to tire now after his great exertions, and made a swift mental count of how many Cats were fighting with each other and how many that left for him to deal with.

Cautiously he circled his two remaining adversaries. They were treating him with a respect equal to his for them. That was, until they heard the rustling approach of two new Cats as they emerged from the bushy forest edge, behind where Jethro stood.

On seeing the approach of their strange fellows, the confidence in the first two Cats immediately arose. This was matched, if not exceeded, by the sinking feeling in Jethro's heart as, now aware of the newcomers, he faced up to bitter prospect of what must be certain defeat.

Worse still, he knew that his and Timmo's families would be lost; doomed either to a cruel death, or transformation into mindless creatures. To add to his predicament the two Cats that Timmo had tied up were gnawing through the rope that secured them and would soon be free to join the others against him.

Whirling around to face these new assailants, it was then, with a feeling of immense relief and joy, that Jethro saw who the newcomers were.

'Thank the stars!' he said to himself, 'Oarskar and Skowt!'

Then aloud he shouted at them, 'Come to my defence, come to my defence my Cats! Attack my foes!'

As he said so he leapt atop the two Cats barely held by Timmo's rope, and, placing a paw on each one's head in turn, completely changed the eventual outcome of the battle in the glade.

Seeing the tide turning in the favour of the

Ticklemouse, the remaining, uncontrolled Cats, realised they were now outnumbered, and sensing imminent defeat soon turned and ran off into the forest at great speed.

With a mock look of great satisfaction and superiority, as demonstrated by the way he twirled his moustaches exaggeratedly, the otter dropped to the ground, and rushed towards Jethro, almost bowling him over in a joyful hug.

'Well done guv, we did it!' he beamed, 'Or, should I say more correctly, you did it!

'Mostly you, of course,' he added. 'Plus those Cats you managed to convert to your way of thinking, and a little, but not insignificant help from 'Yours Truly'.

'Surely if we can manage to win against these beasts,' he went on 'we must stand a fighting chance with the Raiders, if only we can catch up with them!'

'You're right about that,' agreed Jethro, 'The important thing now, though, is to get there in time and I've an idea just how we can do that.'

Chapter 12-

'The Journey To The Sea'

Jethro turned to the twelve Cats under his control and commanded them to lie down, which they did.

Turning back to face Timmo he began to explain,

'Firstly, now we've got these Cats under our control, it makes sense to use them to our advantage.

'They can cover the ground between us and the Raiders in just a few hours, and they're strong enough to carry each of us on their backs, especially if we take turns on different Cats.

'We'll get them to leave us a short distance from the Raiders' encampment, and then order them to lie low in the woods until I call for them to join us.

'You and I can enter the camp as we talked about earlier, and have a good look round.

'Above all, we need to find out where our families are being held captive. Once we know where they are, and hopefully they'll be near to each other, we can order the Cats to launch an attack on the Raiders, and use it as a diversion to release the prisoners and help them to escape.'

'You're right guv,' agreed Timmo, 'and I doubt the Raiders'll be in the mood to follow us after a good maulin' from those Cats over there. They almost give me the 'willies', and I've seen some frightenin' sights in my time.'

'No it's more likely, they'll be too busy makin' for their ships to be interested in resistin' our efforts.'

'Let's be getting along then,' said Jethro as he motioned to Oarskar and Skowt to kneel down and allow himself and Timmo to climb up on to their backs.

The Cats, although returned to normal size, were still strong enough to bear the animals; so, taking a firm grasp of the Cats' shaggy manes, the two companions urged the beasts forward.

As neither Timmo nor Jethro had ever ridden before, it took some distance, and not a little time for them to accustom themselves to this new experience. Oarskar and Skowt gradually picked up speed as they sensed Timmo and Jethro becoming more used to being seated astride them.

The remaining Cats followed, and the whole troop was soon dashing down the moonlit strip of plain, between the woods, and towards the sea.

As Jethro predicted, their progress was much swifter than it would have been if he and Timmo had been on foot. Halfway between midnight and dawn, they reached the tree lined edge of a cliff overlooking the town of *Idloyes* which nestled sleepily on the edge of a small harbour.

A narrow track ran down towards the town on one side. On the other, a wider track ran north westward across the top of the cliff with the sea sparkling under the light of the moon to the right, and the dark mass of the forest to the left.

Turning away from the track leading down to

Idloyes, the party of Cats and their riders headed towards the other path. From their discussions with Nevets the weasel chief and the villagers of *Vale,* they guessed that the Raiders encampment must lay in that direction. Nor were they to be disappointed, as, moving stealthily along the track, they soon rounded a bend at the crest of a hill that overlooked the *Bay of Idloyes.*

Below them stretched out across the grassy dunes, they saw the tents and campfires of the Raiders' landing party. Out in the bay, gently rolling on the swell of the sea as the tide came in, lay the Raiders' ships, five of them in all, night lanterns twinkling and reflecting in rippled surface of the water below.

Dozens of rowing boats, to be used for ferrying the Raiders and their captives back and forth from shore to ship, lay tied up to rocks partly grounded on the beach.

Timmo spoke first, as he and Jethro dismounted from the two Cats that had borne them for the final stage of their race to the sea.

'Looks like we're just in time guv,' he said, 'This tide's goin' to turn at dawn, and they'll be on their way. I never thought in my life, I'd be grateful to a Cat, but without them we'd never have made it.'

'Well, you can thank them properly later when all this is over,' chuckled Jethro, 'right now we need to set the rest of our plan put into action.'

So saying, and under Timmo's instructions, Jethro took the sea rope and shackled the otter. At least that was how it would appear unless anyone got really close to them. In reality, Timmo had only to move his paws in a certain way for the bonds to fall away.

All the time during their latest encounter with the Cats, and during the mad chase to the sea, Jethro had been dressed in the helmet and clothing of a Raider foot soldier. Now with Timmo suitably restrained, the two headed down towards the encampment, apparently jailor and prisoner.

Jethro had given his final instructions to the Cats, telling them to heed his command of 'Come to me!' should it issue either by the sound of his voice or from his mind into their's. He was unsure how far he could project his control by thought, so he also instructed Oarskar and Skowt to watch over the encampment below and to bring the other Cats if he and Timmo appeared to be under attack at any time.

With not a little wariness, the two animals, Timmo in the lead, followed by Jethro occasionally prodding the otter with his sword, as if encouraging a rebellious slave, made their way towards the first sentinel's outpost on the edge of the Raider encampment.
'Oi guv, mind where you're puttin' that cutlass of yours!' hissed Timmo's voice through slightly gritted teeth.

'Sorry Timmo!' whispered Jethro in apology.

As they reached the sentry post, a voice rang out,

'Who approaches the camp of the Raiders? Halt and make yourself known fellow.'

'I bring the otter, incompetently relinquished by Chief Weasel Nevets and his band of moronic fellows.' responded Jethro, trying as best he could to mimic the tones and way of speaking of the Raider sentinel.

He appeared to have succeeded, when the sentinel replied in a pompous voice.

'Welcome brother, your arrival and that of your 'illustrious guest' will be remembered in the future, and written of in glory, when the history of these days is recorded in the Raider Hall of Victory.

'Proceed brother, down to the largest tent in the camp below! Therein are impounded the animal scum we have taken prisoner.'
Jethro prodded Timmo again, mindful of his companion's previous plea for caution, and the two moved slowly down the dunes, towards the centre of the encampment.

Unnoticed by Jethro or Timmo, and to one side of the sentinel's post, hidden in the shadows of the drapes enclosing it, stood

Nevets, a sly look of satisfaction upon his face.

'Well done Sir sentinel, the trap is laid and the General Legin will be more than pleased with us,' he said, an evil smirk spreading over his cruel face, as he watched with glee the unsuspecting pair approach what he knew to be their doom.

Eventually, the two animals arrived in front of the large tent, and, turning into the entrance, slowly and carefully went in.

Barely had they entered and begun to accustom their eyes to the dim light within, than there was a great crash, as a heavy metal cage dropped from above and completely enclosed them.

'Relight the torches!' loudly commanded a chill voice in front and to one side of them.

As the light improved, they looked towards the direction from where the order had come.

Finally, their eyes came to rest on the author of the command, but not before they had taken in the sight of their respective families, looks of anguish and despair upon their faces, chained up not far from where they themselves were caged,

'Welcome Master Ticklemouse, I am the General Legin,' came the cold voice once more, 'I believe you were desirous of a meeting with me?'

'How may I be of service?' continued the voice in a mocking and smug tone.

Chapter 13 –

'The Rescue'

Jethro and Timmo remained silent for a while, as in their own way each of them considered the desperate situation they found both themselves and their respective families in, not to mention the other groups of frightened looking animals, whom their eyes saw as they became further accustomed to the light.

Outside they could hear the first cockerel crow, as dawn began to break over the tree tops of the nearby forest and the sun began to flood onto the Raider encampment.

Jethro eventually signalled to his family with a wave of his paw and a reassuring smile, but Timmo was the first to break their silence.

'Don't you worry Princess, nor you, young Sam!' he said. 'No basket of a Raider's going to hurt you, while I'm around!'

'You speak bravely, Otter, but quite foolishly and pointlessly,' interrupted General Legin.

'Your situation is completely hopeless, and what's more you are powerless against me, in spite of your great strength and bulk. I suggest you hold your tongue, lest your loved ones suffer for your ill chosen outbursts.

'As for you Master Ticklemouse, you are altogether a more thoughtful one, are you not?

'No doubt you are considering using your abilities to control me, but let me disabuse you of that notion. I am immune to them, and so are my soldiers.

'You are wondering, I'm sure, how that can possibly be, as your peculiar *tickling* power can be applied to any animal. So why does it not work on us?

'Sadly, for you that is, you will never know the answer, and soon it will not matter to you. Once I have touched you and the rest of your snivelling kind, you'll become what you were always meant to be: the slaves of my race, here only to provide us with sport or service.

'So now Master Ticklemouse, last of the followers of the Messenger, and Guardian of the Balance, step forward from your cage. Come to me and meet your destiny, but be aware, that one false movement, one aggressive act on your part, and it will be all the worse for your family.'

Turning to Nevets and six of his fellow weasels, General Legin commanded them to open the gate to the cage and lead Jethro and Timmo to him.

As the barred door to the cage opened, the two animals walked docilely towards the weasels, heads bowed in defeat.

All the while, Jethro had been trying to contact the Cats using his mind, unfortunately for him and Timmo, without success. Frustratingly, he realised that the distance between them must be too great for them to communicate with each other.

Slowly, as he approached the weasels, the germ of a plan began to grow in his mind. By the time he was just in front of them, it had flowered into a fully fledged course of action.

In an instant, whilst seeming to stumble clumsily, he half fell and half leapt forward onto them, touching each of their foreheads so fast that General Legin and his soldiers were completely unaware of what he was doing.

Suddenly Timmo, who was following behind Jethro, was hurled by the group of weasels through the entrance of the tent to the outside. Jethro had just instructed the Weasels to attack the otter.

From their vantage point looking down on the Raider encampment, the vigilant Cats saw their master's companion burst through the tent wall followed by seven vicious looking Weasels armed with clubs and spears, and clearly intent upon doing the otter harm.

Oarskar and Skowt immediately leap forward, urging their fellows into action with hisses and growls.

'To the Master and the Otter!' commanded Skowt, as she and Oarskar, followed by the rest of the Cats, hurtled down the hill towards the encampment, all the time emitting the most hideous screams and roars, as, once again, they grew to a more formidable size.

It took them no time to reach the large tent, outside of which, Timmo, having quickly shed his bonds, was busy defending himself against Raider soldier and weasel alike.

At the sight of the savage Cats racing towards them, many of the Raiders dropped their weapons and made for the boats on the beach. The weasels just ran to wherever they could, hoping to find shelter.

Inside the tent, Jethro advanced towards General Legin, who was beginning to turn away from him. Jethro's heart was bursting with joy at the turn of events, and, as he thought of their possible impending victory over the Raiders, the beginnings of a smile played upon his face.

Without warning, he leapt high into the air and over General Legin's head. Twisting as he landed so as to place himself in front of the chained animals, he turned to face General Legin and his troops, and spoke.

'I may not be able to control your mind or those of your fellows, General Legin,' he began, 'but I'm willing to wager that I can preoccupy you just long enough for the Cats to get here. And you don't much care for them, I understand, do you?

'As for working your evil tricks on me, I'm equally confident that if I can't control you, the reverse is true, and any attempt you make to transform me will meet with failure.'

Beneath the helmet that covered most of it, General Legin's hairless face flushed with anger, and he said with a snarl, 'You may have won this time Ticklemouse, but we'll meet again, and when we do I swear by the dark void, you'll be sorry!'

At that, he and his immediate guards ran out of the tent, avoiding as best they could, the raking talons of the Cats and Timmo's bludgeoning tail.

Using both his long arms and short legs to good effect, General Legin propelled himself forward in a low, crouching gallop towards the beach and the tethered boats.

As he reached the nearest waiting craft, he leapt aboard, just as the few remaining survivors of his personal guard were preparing to shove the vessel out into the water, before springing onboard it themselves.

Back on the shore, the Cats, under Jethro's control, had rounded up the remaining Raiders and Weasels and, by forming a ring around them, kept their vanquished foes captive.

From the tent Jethro could see the sandy beach littered with the slain bodies of the Raiders and Weasels alike.

He regretted the death of any creature, however evil, but he had been unable to regain control of the Cats quickly enough to prevent the carnage.

He and Timmo's first instinct, once it was clear that the Raiders were in retreat, was to release the chained up animals and re-unite themselves with their families.

Naturally they were all overjoyed. Gem and Ash danced around Nana, singing with excitement, while Jethro and Hanna embraced each other in relief.

Elsewhere in the tent, Timmo's great arms encircled Linith and Sam, in a loving hug. The three animals were visibly moved by their reunion, not having seen each other for so long.

The remaining captives formed in groups of families and friends, some mourning the loss of loved ones, others joyful at being together again, and free from the yoke of the Raiders.

Timmo, half carrying his family along with him, walked over to where the Ticklemice stood.

'Linith, Sam, let me introduce you to Jethro,' he said as they approached the Ticklemouse and his family.

'The last few days have very much reminded me of my days on the high seas, and Jethro here would've made a more than worthy shipmate.'

As if to reinforce his remark, there came the sound of canon fire out in the bay. Concerned that it might be the Raiders returning, every animal, adult and young, left what they were doing and rushed to the seashore to find out what was happening.

At the northern extremity of the *Idloyes* bay where the open sea began, the group of animals saw two of the Raiders' ships heading towards the east. The remaining three crewless ships, heaved on their anchor chains as the ebbing tide ran out to sea.

The canon fire had come from a vessel approaching from the south east, clearly bearing the colours of the marine militia.

A huge cheer rose from Timmo's throat,

'By the spirit and all that's good, they did come,' he said. 'My old shipmates must have got my message.

'Give it to them lads,' he roared, 'let 'em know what it feels like to be on the receivin' end for a change.'

Further fire issued from the ship upon which Timmo's shipmates sailed. Such was the accuracy of their aim that, soon, the central mast of the nearer Raider vessel collapsed, to be swiftly followed by a disabling shot to its rudder.

The stricken craft was quickly reached by the militia boat and boarded by the fearless squadron of sailors.

By this time the second Raider ship, with General Legin aboard, had gained the open water and with sails full of wind, was speeding eastwards out of reach of its pursuers.

Chapter 14 –

'Raiders Revealed?'

Although the events of the previous day and night had been long and arduous, Timmo and Jethro felt not the least bit tired. Their spirits and energy were raised up by the great happiness brought about by seeing their families safe and well. However, for Timmo, Linith and Samwell the joy of finding each other again was lessened somewhat by the mourning of their beloved Sophar, who would stay in their minds and hearts forever.

Later that day, the Captain of the mariners, a sea otter almost as imposing as Timmo, came ashore with some of the retired mariner's former shipmates, which assisted in distracting him from dwelling too long on his tragic loss.

After much good-natured banter between Timmo and his mates, and at the Captain's suggestion, a service was held to remember and honour those who had fallen during the Raiders' hateful visit to their shores.

Many of the animals prayed aloud to the Great Spirit. Those unconvinced of the existence of a universal force for good, said a silent goodbye to their fallen comrades or loved ones.

Afterwards, these former prisoners of the Raiders turned to wondering anxiously how they would manage on return to their respective villages.

But the villagers need not have worried for the abandoned Raiders' ships contained much of what they had plundered and carried off, and it was decided that each villager should be given a share of these spoils.

In this way, all were provided with sufficient stores to see them through the coming winter. As if this were not enough, further sacks of a variety of seeds were given to them. These were intended to be sown immediately on their return, and would be ready for harvest in the Spring and Summer of the following year. Any personal items that the villagers could identify as their's, were also returned to them.

Each village was allocated one of the many abandoned wagons used by the Raiders to transport their plunder. These the villagers used to load their belongings and the supplies onto.

Other wagons were to be used for carrying the aged and injured on the return journey to their homes.

As evening approached, the animals began drawing together in village groups, rekindling fires and preparing their evening meals.

By the time night had fallen, the surviving inhabitants of *Vale* and of Timmo's village, which they now knew was called *Felday*, congregated around several small fires.

Timmo, Jethro and their families sat together with the Captain of the mariners, and, after everyone had finished their supper and the youngsters had been packed off to bed, they each began to fill in the gaps in the other's knowledge of the events leading up to the battle with the Raiders.

Jethro told them of the discovery of the scroll and its contents, together with a brief but modest account of his gifts, and how he had been able to use them over the past few days.

It then fell to the Captain to relate the details of the marine militia's encounter with the Raiders.

'Your note to us could not have been better timed, Timmo,' he began, 'We'd been receiving reports for sometime of these so called Raiders and their evil deeds. But it seemed as if every time we got close to them they would just vanish into thin air.

'So it was a blessing when that brave little bird of yours landed exhausted onto our deck, the morning before last.

'Fortunately, we were less than a day's sail from here, and the opportunity to help you out whilst giving the Raiders a bloody nose, was too good to resist.

'We made much better time than expected, thanks to a following wind, as well as sailing through the night, and, Spirit be praised, we

arrived just in time to give the baskets what
they deserved.'

'Yeah,' interrupted Timmo, 'great it was. We
were all watching and cheering from the
shore. You might have heard us?'

'To be truthful, Timmo,' continued the
Captain, 'I can't say as I did. We were too
busy dealing with the Raiders.'

'Fought like Cats they did, and it took us a
while to subdue them. Unfortunately, not
before their officer in charge had transformed
some of the crew into mindless misshapen
creatures.

'Of course we'd heard about this frightening
ability that their leaders possess, but
nonetheless it was still a shock actually seeing
it happen.

'Fortunately one of the crew cottoned on to
the fact that the Raider officers alone could
do it and then only by touching the poor
animal they wanted to transform. So we
lassoed him and roped the blighter up to the
main mast, where he could do no more harm.

'First of all he was foulmouthed as could be, called us all sorts, some I'd never heard before, made even the first mate blush.

'Anyway, after a while all the fight seems to go out of him and seeing how angry and vengeful the crew were, what with some of their shipmates having suffered so, he commences pleading with me for his life.

'"What do we get in return?" I ask him.

'"That which you are not in possession of," he replies, looking all sly and cunning "Information."

'"Alright," says I, "you talk and we'll see if what you've to say is worth your scurvy life. First up, what are you and your mates up to, apart from stealing and killing? What's your game Raider my lad?"

'At that he composes himself and starts to speak, taking on a very superior tone.

'"We are a species different from any known to you lower order creatures. We are not of your animal kingdom. We are the Homenim and our allegiance is to the Dark Spirit."

"'We are his instruments on this world and we are here to prepare and plan the way for his arrival, and ultimate supreme reign. Our first intention was to send a reconnaissance party here, to gauge what sort of resistance we might expect and how easy it would be to transform you into a form useful to us as slaves or food."

"'Matters were proceeding in accordance with our plans, until," he said sneeringly, "this *Master* Ticklemouse and that over zealous Otter friend of his arrived with their Cats and interfered."

"'Unhappily for us this interference has caused a temporary set back, but our leader, the General Legin, is not without guile himself, and will no doubt regroup our forces for further attacks on you and your brethren. Not to mention that this is the first time that he has suffered defeat and it will not sit well with him. Rest assured that he will not leave the accounting unsettled. His return will be accompanied by an even larger force and when he does return, you will be driven, like the vermin you are, back to your lodges and burrows only to await your ultimate transformation into the Dark Spirit's minions."

'Then he fell silent.' resumed the Captain, 'couldn't get a nod, let alone another word out of him, no matter how much we threatened him with all kinds of consequences.

'It seemed as though him speaking about his *Homenim* and the *Dark Spirit*, the way he did, all arrogant and superior, had given him some spine back.

'Anyway he and his mates are chained up in the brig now, where they won't do anymore damage'

Jethro, who had been waiting patiently to speak ever since he'd heard the first mention of *Homenim*, was finally able to do so as the Captain finished.

'Well I suppose that pretty much clears up everything,' he said. 'And it answers something that's been puzzling me since yesterday.'

'I know it sounds funny but I heard my father's voice,' he went on, explaining about how he used to have a phobia for birds, 'and he told me that I need fear no creature, fowl, animal or homenim.'

'I wondered what in the Great Spirit's name a 'homenim' was and now, thanks to you Captain, I know.

'That also explains in part why their transformation powers won't work on me. Since, if I have nothing to fear from them, then that can only mean these powers are ineffective in my case.'

'What will happen to them?' he asked the Captain.

'Well, come the morning tide,' replied the mariner, 'we'll hoist sail and take them and their ships, together with what remains of their ill gotten spoils back to the Capital. Then they'll be tried for their crimes and the Wise Ones will decree their fate after that.'

'Talking of the Wise Ones, they'll probably

want to call a gathering of all the town and village heads, to discuss what we're to do about any future threat from these Raiders or Homenim as they call themselves.

'I expect you and Timmo will be called to give evidence against them at their trial, and no doubt the council of the gathering will want to hear your thoughts about any measures we might take to prepare for their return.

'Especially you Jethro, given these talents you appear to have developed. Not many will have heard of the Ticklemice, and even less will know of the Guardians of the Messenger, that you've been telling me about. No doubt, you'll have a lot of explaining to do to the Wise Ones.

'And now with your leave gentle folk, I'll retire to my bed, it's been a long old day, and it'll be an early rise for us, if we're to catch the ebb tide right.'

With that, each of them went into the tent that contained their family or fellows and lay down, most sleeping a peaceful dreamless sleep.

Chapter 15 –

'Home At Last!'

Early the next morning Timmo, Jethro and their families, stood waving on the shore as the mariner's ship headed for the open seas. It was followed by the remaining Raider ships which were helmed by 'skeleton' crews, each ship being partly towed by the one ahead of it to assist them.

By mid morning all the wagons were loaded, and the different groups of villagers began to head back to their homes.

Each set of travellers was accompanied by a Cat, the number of which, by good fortune, was sufficient for this purpose. The Cats were under Jethro's orders to guide their charges unharmed through the dangerous territories that were home to the Cats, and then to leave the villagers to carry on alone to complete the rest of their journey without fear of attack.

The party with which, Jethro, Timmo, and their families travelled, was flanked front and rear by Oarskar and Skowt. The former lead them at a leisurely pace back up towards the waterfall junction and the source of the two rivers.

In comparison to their hectic rescue journey, which was completed in hours, the return passage took all of two days.

By the time they had reached Timmo's boat, it had been decided that the Ticklemice, with Timmo and his family, would camp near the damaged boat, so that he and Jethro could set about returning the vessel to a seaworthy state.

The villagers of *Vale* and *Felday* continued on their separate ways, shepherded by Oarskar and Skowt. When each group was safely out of Cat country, both Cats left to return to Timmo and Jethro's camp.

With a good supply of materials at hand, and using Timmo's sea chest of boat tools, the craft was repaired in a few days, and was ready for their departure.

For the last part of their enforced stay to rectify the damage to the boat, the Cats had been with them. The three youngsters in particular had taken to play fighting with them and were sad when the time for parting came.

'Oh Dada,' cried Gem and Ash, 'Pleeeese, pleeeese, can't we take Oarskar and Skowt home with us?'

'I'm afraid not my ducks,' he replied with a tinge of sadness in his voice. 'It wouldn't be fair on them.

'They love to roam their own wild lands, and can you imagine the commotion it would cause in the village, having two ferocious animals on our fields. Folks would be too frightened to leave their homes.

'We've a lot to thank them for though, and I know I'll never forget them, neither will Mummy. Will you love?' he said, turning to his wife.

'No, I shall always have them in my thoughts, especially as they saved Daddy's life,' she replied giving Jethro a warm hug.

'Anyway,' she continued 'I've some news that might make up for the Cats leaving. I'm

in the family way again, and the baby should arrive just before the Spirit Tide festival.'
'Oh great Mama,' cried Gem gleefully, 'I only hope it's not another brother.'

'Oi you!' said Ash. 'What's wrong with brothers?'

'I just don't know where to begin!' said his sister disdainfully.

'Calm down' said Hanna. 'We don't know what it's going to be, and as long as the baby's healthy, I'm sure we don't care.

I'm not sure we could cope with another like Gem, though,' she said teasingly, winking at Jethro.

Now it was Gem's turn to say 'Oi, Mamaaa!' in an offended tone.

In a while, the children said goodbye to the Cats, followed by Timmo and Linith. Last of all, Jethro and Hanna approached and embraced each in turn.

'We really won't ever forget you,' said Hanna.

'We will always return at the Master's bidding,' purred Oarskar.

'But now we must leave and rejoin our fellows,' said Skowt, and with that the two Cats turned and departed.

'Well,' said Timmo breaking into the silence that had descended on the scene at the Cat's departure, 'she's ready to go.'

'It'll be a bit of a squeeze, but I've cleared out the fore cabin for the Ladies, and as long as they behave, the young uns can stay with us by the ship's wheel. Might even let 'em have a go at the wheel, if they're really good!'

With all their supplies loaded, the animals boarded the small craft, took their places and waited whilst Timmo and Jethro cast off at each end.

The two animals hauled the sails and slowly the boat began to move towards the riverhead, in the direction they had come from a few days ago.

'We should make better time on the way back,' said Timmo, 'We'll have the downstream current with us and the wind seems to be changing to a north easterly. We'll be in for some snow soon. Mark my words!'

And he was right, about both things. They reached the City in a little over a day, stopping just long enough to take on supplies and medicine for Nana, before carrying on downstream.

Two days later they moored up close to the spot where Timmo and Jethro had first met.

'Looks like goodbye then,' said Timmo hesitantly.

Before he could go on, Jethro interrupted him.

'Well, perhaps not,' he began. 'Hanna and I have been talking and we've a suggestion to make.'

'We thought that, as winter's nearly upon us and your lodge probably needs a fair bit of work doing on it to make it habitable, you might like to stay with us until Spring. Then you, I and Samwell, could go down to *Felday* and sort things out.'

Timmo looked at Linith quizzically, an eyebrow raised.

'What d'you reckon, Memsab?' he enquired.

'Do you honestly need me to answer?' asked Linith. 'Of course I'd love to, it would be really wonderful.'

'Yes please,' she said turning to Hanna and Jethro, 'and thanks for everything Jethro, he'd be dead now if it weren't for you.'

'No thanks needed Linith, I owe Timmo just as much, believe me. He's saved my skin more than a few times, he's a great chap.'

Timmo and Jethro made the 'Buckler' fast, ensuring that the mooring was secure enough to last for the coming winter. As they did so the first light flakes of snow began to fall.

'We'd better be off before this sets in,' said Jethro.

By evening they were at the Ticklemice home, settling in for what ended up being the coldest, longest winter in living memory.

Fortunately, in addition to the supplies that they had recovered from the Raiders' storage holds, Jethro was extremely pleased to find his underground food store had - despite the Raiders presence - remained hidden and thus untouched, during the abduction of his family. There would be more than enough for them all including Nana, Grammy and Grampa.

The days that followed passed in blissful peace for all the animals, who became even closer friends than they had been at the end of their recent adventures with the Raiders.

Eventually, just before Spirit Tide, Hanna's baby arrived, and was delivered by Jethro using his newly acquired skills. The Ticklemice decided to call the baby, who was a female, Iba, meaning gift of the Spirit.

The next few days were very busy as everyone prepared for the Spirit Tide feast. The whole house was adorned with holly, mistletoe and ivy.

The holly was particularly beautiful, as it was covered in red and gold berries, which complemented the silver white berries of the mistletoe.

On the feast day the stout oak table in the Ticklemice household positively groaned under the weight of food and drink.
There were acorn pies, cheese and coriander soup with braised onions, and the centre piece was a fresh wild pink salmon caught by Timmo the day before, poached in elderflower and dill sauce.

The whole was rounded off by Spirit Tide pudding: a mixture of nuts, berries and flour all soaked in peach brandy, steamed in a basin and then served with custard and cream.

For the adults, there was elderberry wine and chilled sparkling elderflower to drink, as well as burdock beer. The youngsters contented themselves with a concoction of rosehip syrup mixed with ginger beer and lemonade.

After the meal they exchanged simple but meaningful presents, before, in the case of the

Ticklemice children, going upstairs with the inevitable mischief in mind, and in the adult animals' case clearing up the remains of the celebration.

Later that evening as Linith and Hanna were reading stories to their children upstairs, Timmo and Jethro retired to the living room, where a fire blazed welcomingly in the hearth.

'You know I've been thinking,' said Timmo, 'after all the adventures we've had recently, things might get a bit borin'. Wouldn't you agree guv'?'

'I must say Timmo, I'm not complaining,' said Jethro, yawning slightly as he curled up in his armchair in front of the roaring fire, 'A bit of peace and quiet for a while wouldn't come amiss.'

The two animals remained silent for some moments, as if dozing, when suddenly Timmo broke their reverie.

'Didn't you say you'd got some kids somewhere the other side of Raider country?

and that you haven't seen them for ages?'

'Er yes,' said Jethro cautiously.
'Well??' asked Timmo with a twinkle in his eye.

'We'll talk about it. After we've fixed your lodge up. Possibly.....' replied Jethro.

The End